# Saint Knickers

## E. V Faulkner

Sticks & Stones

First published in Great Britain in 2023 by
Sticks & Stones

All content © E.V Faulkner, 2023

ISBN: 9798854679831

The moral right of E.V Faulkner to be identified as the author of this work has been asserted in accordance with the Copyright, Designs and Patents Act, 1988. All rights reserved. No part of this publication may be reproduced or transmitted in any form or by any means, electronic or mechanical, including photocopy, recording, or any information storage and retrieval system, without permission in writing from the publisher. This book is a work of fiction. Names, characters, businesses, organisations, places and events are either the product of the author's imagination or are used fictitiously. Any resemblance to actual persons, living or dead, events or locales is entirely coincidental.

First Edition

Book design by Alexandra Peel

ACKNOWLEDGMENTS

This is for all the

Miss Sparrows, Nurse Halifaxs, Mr Wrights and Aunty Nells out there.

*'A virtuous character is likened to an unblemished flower. Piety is a fadeless bud that half opens on earth and expands through eternity. Sweetness of temper is the odor of fresh blooms, and the amaranth flowers of pure affection open but to bloom forever.'*
*Dorothea Dix*

Saint Peter's Knickers

'Piety Scroggins ate a pie
Piety Scroggins is going to die
Piety Scroggins smells like sick
Piety Scroggins is thick, thick, thick!'

England, 1975,

"I wonder what colour undies Jesus wore?"

They looked thoughtfully, from their prone positions on the playing field, at the slow-moving clouds as though the answer might appear there miraculously. The grass was both soft and spiky. The subtle aroma of squashed green surrounded them. A woven daisy chain lay abandoned and wilting on a divested navy cardigan. A wittering sparrow darted by. One of those days when sleep came easily beneath the sun and the soft caress of air carried the scent of fresh mown grass, earth, crab apple and hawthorn flowers — promises of eternal days of childhood. Late spring.

"Jesus didn't wear underwear, idiot."
"' Course, he did. Everyone wears knickers or

underpants."
"Not in those days. My dad said they just let their peckers swing free."
"What's a pecker?"
"You know," Aaron sat up and pointed at his crotch. "Your dick."

The group giggled. Piety chortled. If anyone were going to say a rude word, it would be Aaron Brockley. Richard Burns repeated the word between peals of laughter, *dick, dick, dick.*

"What are you laughing at, Scroggy Scroggins?" Aaron stood.

Piety reclined on the grass six feet from the small gaggle. She was not part of their group. She was not part of any group. He took a step closer to her.

"Scraggy Scroggins, more like," Richard Burns cackled.
"Pooh!" Nicole Samson held her tiny nose and wafted her hand. "Smells like puke."
"Did you puke, Scroggy?" demanded Aaron.

She shook her head and recoiled.

Richard joined him, "I bet you did. I bet you puked all down your uniform and into your shoes. That's why you stink so much."

Aaron made exaggerated vomiting noises. He pretended to puke on the grass, on his friends and finally, on Piety. Huge great heaves and belches making her scrabble backwards, scooting her bottom on the grass. Eight eyes bored into her. She could feel the heat searing through her shabby navy sweater and discoloured shirt. Piety left.

"Piety Scroggins smells like sick, Piety Scroggins is thick, thick, thick!"

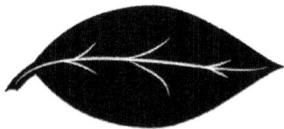

# Part One

# Chapter One

Piety's parents did not believe in God. Nor did they believe in Heaven. She knew this because Dad would scoff at people on TV who talked about religion, and Mum would say if God existed, why didn't he let them live in a bigger and better bloody house? If God existed, why did he let shit happen? But they did send her and her little brother to the local Sunday School. She liked singing. She liked colouring pictures of bible stories. She liked the walk there – holding Tommy's little chubby hand in hers as he chatted away in his unintelligible toddler speak. Sunday School was divided by age, a bit like real school. There were Infant classes and Junior classes. Once you reached the age of twelve or thirteen, you went to proper church - or you could help with the little kids. Piety thought she might like this. Mum and Dad must want her to be religious even if they weren't, she reasoned. Or did they want her soul to be saved because it was too late for them? She pondered all this as she traipsed home alone.

She took off her cardigan and tied it around her

waist, the arms looped over and over each other, because she wasn't good at tying knots. It was turning into a warm day. The strap of her schoolbag chafed against the side of her neck and collarbone. She scratched the itch. Her socks kept slipping down because the elastic had gone in them, but she repeatedly paused to hitch them up.

The route from Beacon Park Primary School took Piety along a main road, lined with detached houses Piety thought massive. She was sure the front gardens alone were bigger than her whole house. The next ones were semis, which had smaller gardens at the front. On the corner of Kirk Road, *her* road, stood a big rotten house that was not attached to its neighbour. The garden swept around the whole side of it and huge twisty trees grew there. She kept her head down, eyes on the paving stones. Everyone knew the old woman who lived there stole kids. Very rarely was she seen in the rambling garden hanging clothes on a line strung between a couple of crooked trees. Piety hurried past, for the old house took up a disproportionate amount of her route; because it was on the corner, and its tangled garden was much larger than anyone else's. If you didn't look, you could pretend that the witch house wasn't there, or that someone was watching from an upstairs window — planning their next meal.

The houses grew smaller giving way to blocks of tatty terraces, newer than those on the main road, but they did not have gardens; front or back. Each terrace was separated from the pavement by a low wall one stride from the front door. Kids would sit on the walls, kicking their feet, leaning back against someone's window, scraping jagged stick figures into the stonework. Some had gates, but most did not. A few residents had put potted plants in the narrow gap beneath the front window. Her house had nothing — except crisp and sweet wrappers, cigarette butts and empty packets.

"Pee pee Piety!"

She looked across to the opposite side of the road. Two boys whom she did not know, sang their taunts.

"Pie, Pie, fatty Pie. Ate a dog is gonna die."
"That doesn't even make sense," Piety giggled.

The boys laughed. She thought they might be in the year below her, but couldn't be sure. They continued shouting insults and chants. Piety stopped walking and faced them across the tarmac.

"Sticks and stones will break my bones and names will never hurt me!" She felt confident this was a clever and appropriate response.

They fetched stones from the gutter and pelted her with them. When she still hadn't responded to their satisfaction, they pulled twigs from the sparse privet hedges and darted across the road. They lunged and poked at her as though she was some sort of wild beast in a cage. And didn't stop until she turned through the rust-scabbed gate which resisted and complained when opened. One stride to the front door and in.

"Why'd you bring them kids?"

Mum was kneeling up on her chair, holding back the net curtain.
"I didn't. They followed me."

But Mum simply made a *tutting* noise, rolled her eyes, and turned back to her big puzzle book. It was no use explaining it wasn't her fault. Why were the boys so mean? she wondered. She hadn't done anything to them, crikey, she didn't know them.

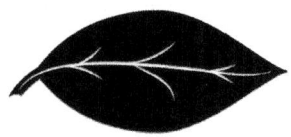

At five years of age, Piety had come to the decision that she wanted to be a mermaid when she grew up. When it was announced to Class 4S they would begin swimming lessons, she was thrilled. Because the leisure centre was so far away, the school only made one trip per year, plus, they would be getting a coach there! Piety had never been on a coach before and could not contain her excitement. She jumped up and down and ran in circles — so much energy couldn't be contained for a whole journey. Thirty-two eight and nine-year-olds gabbled excitedly as they clamoured to board the coach first.

"Stay in line everyone," called Miss Sparrow. "Aaron, calm down, please."

Aaron had a new Scalextric for his birthday and the boys converged on him to goggle and admire the car he had brought in. Nicole and Kaylee knelt on their seats facing backwards so that they could talk to the two girls sitting behind them. Carol Beverley went right to the back with Fiona and Helen, but Piety thought it smelt like fumes and it made her feel queasy. Miss said she should sit at the front — in case she felt sick. No one sat next to Piety, so she put her bag on the seat beside her. She stared out of the window, watching the houses and shops, the Town Hall and patches of bare land surrounded by mesh railings. The familiar soon transformed into the unknown. More traffic, less housing, a road that went over the one they were on — Miss Sparrow told them it was called a flyover. The clouds were huge and puffy, and Piety thought it would be lovely to sit on one.

"Miss Sparrow."
"Yes, Piety?"
"What do clouds feel like?"
The teacher looked puzzled momentarily. "Why do you ask?"
"I was thinking how lovely it would be to sit on one. Do you think they are soft like the pillows on that advert on TV?"

Someone behind her sniggered.
Miss Sparrow gave it some thought. "Well, clouds are made from water droplets, so I imagine one would get awfully wet, don't you?"

Piety considered this. She couldn't imagine how water stayed in such fluffy shapes, like white candy floss. Surely, they weren't *really* made of water. Could Miss have made a mistake? She didn't think so, teachers knew everything. So, she simply nodded and continued looking at the world passing by, jiggling her feet, and breathing 'huh' on the window to draw little stars and faces.

At the pool, she couldn't wait to get in the water. Everyone had to queue up for a basket to keep their personal belongings in. Piety kept stepping out of line to see what was happening. Some of the kids said they had been here before and talked as though they knew the assistants, with that cocky self-assuredness that seemed to be like well-fitting clothes. Piety thanked the staff as they handed out baskets and directions to the changing rooms. She jiggled from one foot to the other with anticipation; Carol Beverley elbowed her and asked if she needed a wee. The place echoed. And it smelt strange. Piety had never visited a public pool before and had not realised that it would smell so different to anywhere else she had been. It wasn't exactly an unpleasant smell, Miss said it was chlorine, used to keep the water clean. Piety's giggle turned into a snorting guffaw — amazed that the stuff that washed things could be washed. She could barely contain her excitement, getting in the water was going to be brilliant.

They trooped along the edge of the swimming pool to the changing rooms that lined it. Everyone was wittering and twittering, a great chorus of starling-kids on their maiden flight. She ripped off her clothes and wriggled into her swimsuit, bumping elbows and knees against the walls of the confined space. She stuffed everything into the funny mesh basket. There was a metal hook on the wall, but she didn't bother with that. She left her school bag on the floor of the cubicle. Dashed out to join everyone at the poolside. There was a balcony that went all around the walls and two big signs saying Deep End and Shallow End. The ceiling was all painted metal crossbars and glass, through which she could see the white sky. Light shone on the lovely dark green tiles that covered the walls. Like a palace, she beamed.

Someone made a funny snorting sound. Another sounded like a raspberry. Giggling and titters rippled through the pale-skinned shivering class. Piety giggled along; everyone was as giddy with anticipation as she was.

"Best day ever," she said to no one in particular, shivering in the lofty, wide space.

Her swimming costume had not been new when her mum bought it. The original blue had faded to a bleached off-green in parts and there was a hole over her right buttock.

"Piety's got a hole in her bum, Miss!"

The class roared with laughter. The instructor at the pool ushered her quickly into the water, but the other kids complained that she was turning the water brown. She sucked a huge breath as the freezing water rose up her body.

"'Cos she never gets a bath at home!"
This wasn't true, Piety told them, she did bathe. "Every two weeks, whether I need it or not," she replied in jest.

In truth, Piety could not remember when she last had a bath. Occasionally, she used the pink rubber shower attachment that was stuck on the bath taps. Mostly, she washed at the sink, with the yellow flannel that used to be white. But she once heard someone say 'whether I need it or not' on TV, and the audience laughed. But her classmates did not laugh. They made faces and waded to the opposite side. Piety thought this was rather mean of them, but what hurt the most was that Carol Beverley — her best friend, did not stick by her. Weren't friends meant to stick together? She tried not to care, but it was hard to have fun on your own in a pool with thirty-one other kids.

Miss Sparrow did not get into the water. Piety was a little disappointed about this at first, but quickly forgot about her teacher as the instructor had them practising the breaststroke and the crawl. Some of her classmates did backstroke. She looked on with admiration. Their arms rose in rainbow plumes, cycling back and back. Feet appearing and disappearing in wet ruffles. She just couldn't keep her chin above the water, no matter how hard she paddled. She snorted enormous amounts which stung the inside of her nose and made her cough and laugh, which made her snort even more. Her hair got in her eyes and each time she stopped to push it away, she slowly sank. There was a huge amount of splashing, which was great fun — no one else could splash the way she did. As long as she could keep her toes on the bottom all was well, but she was not allowed in the Deep End until she could swim better. She gulped so much that she imagined that she drank more water than she ever had before in her life and felt a bit sick. The best bit was holding onto the stone edge and stretching her legs out behind and kicking like mad.

The instructor had some blue plastic armbands which you were allowed to wear. A lot of the kids wore them, but Piety pulled on two pairs. Aaron Brockley didn't need anything to help him float, but when he put them on his ankles and tipped backwards, everyone thought it was hilarious. Piety laughed as hard as the others as he splashed and sloshed about — until she realised that he was play-acting when he shouted,

"Help, help, I'm Scroggy and I can't swim!"

She felt the smile slip from her face as some of the kids looked at her, wet eyes and lips gleaming like polished glass. Others couldn't swim, she wasn't the only one. Why did he have to use her name?

It was all over very quickly, it seemed. Piety could have stayed there all day — until her whole body was as wrinkly as her fingers. Her hands were pale as cheese and her thighs were covered in tiny goose bumps. Everyone shivered and chattered as they dashed back to their respective cubicles. That was when Piety realised that she had forgotten a towel. What should she do? Borrow one? But who from? She stood in the stall cold-wobbling, wet hands tucked into wet armpits, looking at the wash of pool water that had invaded the floor, soaking her bag and belongings. In the end, she opted to use her school shirt and fasten the buttons of her cardigan so that no one would see it was wet.

"Where's your coat, Piety?" Miss Sparrow counted everyone as they boarded the coach.
"I haven't got one, Miss." The teacher looked upset.

"It's okay, I have one for wintertime. It's spring now so I don't need one yet."
"But your hair's soaking. Didn't you dry it properly? You'll catch a cold."
"Hurry up!" Kaylee Jones shoved Piety's back.
"That was fun, Miss." Piety said when they were almost back at school.
"I'm glad you enjoyed it, Piety."
"When can we go again?"
"Well, that depends on timetables. And all the other classes need a turn, so I'm not sure."
"Oh." Piety looked out of the window, hoping it wouldn't be too long until the next swimming session. She'd try to remember a towel next time.

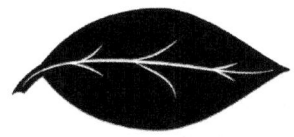

Piety had what the school nurse called 'a weak bladder'. She went at least once a week to the nurse's office for clean underwear. Miss Halifax kept a collection of miscellaneous clothing and school shoes and pumps. These were the things that had sat in Lost Property for ages and ages. Because nobody claimed them, they ended up in the nurse's office. Piety looked at the shelves of half-folded shirts and stacks of shoes and pairs of pumps secured with elastic bands. Such a lot of lost clothing, how could anyone go home without their shoes? She had a giggle at this.

"Have you been drinking a lot at break time, Piety?" Miss Halifax asked as she rummaged in the ugly

green, metal cupboard.
She pulled out a pair of boy's shorts, apologising that she didn't have any girl's underwear available. The school nurse didn't talk like anyone Piety knew; she sounded like she was sort of singing when she talked — Miss Sparrow said she was from a place called Wales. She had deep brown hair which she always wore wavy, that shone as though it had been polished. The plain blue uniform didn't conceal the rise of her breasts or the heft of her hips. She was all curvy, not like Piety's mum. She wondered what it would be like to be hugged by the curvy woman. A tiny mothlike memory flickered and was gone.

"No, Miss." Piety removed her damp knickers, which Nurse Halifax put into a plastic bag for her, and pulled on the shorts. They were a bit baggy around the waist. "I never need to go to the toilet at break time, only when we get back to class, and you're not allowed to leave the classroom, no matter how many times you ask, and sometimes it just comes out 'cos I can't hold it for hours and hours. Even when I wiggle on my chair."
"Has your mum taken you to see your GP?" Piety stared. "The doctor Piety, have you seen a doctor?" She put a safety pin in the back of the waistband to stop the pants slipping down.

Piety shook her head. Miss Halifax had one of those bright, open friendly faces. She always smiled when she passed you in the corridor. She always said good morning in her lovely sing-song voice. But not now. Her brow had a little crease, and her mouth wasn't smiling. She breathed a heavy sigh before patting Piety's shoulder and sending her off.

When she returned to class, the caretaker was mopping beneath her desk. Carol Beverley did not look up from her writing as Piety retook her seat next to her. Fiona and Helen, who sat opposite, had their chairs pushed back so that the puddle could be swabbed. Miss Sparrow instructed the class to continue working, but everyone watched her walk back to her seat and watched the caretaker until he left carrying the mop and metal bucket.
"Only babies wee their pants," Fiona whispered to Helen.

But it was loud enough for Piety to hear. That stung a little. She wasn't a baby; she was eight and a half. She couldn't help it; she didn't do it deliberately. She was just hanging on for too long.

She stopped drinking at school. She became terribly thirsty so that when she arrived home, she stuck her mouth to the kitchen sink tap and guzzled until her stomach was a firm ball.

"Pi! Stop drinking so much! You'll piss the bed again!"

At school, she became known as Pee-Pee Piety.

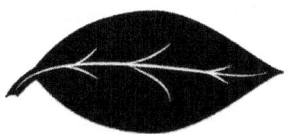

The backyard of Piety's house was exactly eight by

ten feet in size. She knew this because Billy Ramsey down the road had told her when she was hanging around the back entryway once. She asked him what he was doing when she saw loads of wood being dragged in, he was rebuilding his pigeon coop — his yard and the wall were iced with droppings. In the Scroggins' yard, there were lumps of discarded toys that recorded the ages of the two children that lived there; a broken plastic buggy, a tricycle with a wheel missing, damaged dolls, pieces of plastic train track, and a baby's dummy wedged into the folds of cheap carpet. Torn refuse sacks and mouldering food spilt from the metal bin. Everything was damp and stinking and coated with a smattering of sickly yellow lichen. No flowers. No ornaments. No grass. Sometimes one of the teachers would say that they had spent the weekend in the garden. Piety wished she had a garden like the houses along the main road. But no one around here did. All the long rows of terraces had identical backyards paved in identical grey-brown flags, hemmed in by identical high red brick walls. There was a song that sometimes played on the radio — little ticky-tacky houses all looking just the same, that must have been about here, she decided.

When Piety opened the back door one day and stood on the step facing the wall that was the divider between theirs and old Mrs Thompson's, she saw a green thing sticking from between the russet bricks where the mortar was crumbling. A single shoot curled against the redness, and as far as she could tell, it was healthy. She watched a grey bug trundle past; Piety did not know this thing was called a woodlouse. She wondered vaguely what it was thinking about and if insects thought about anything at all. Did dogs and cats think about things? Probably about food and getting strokes and pats. She considered whether plants had thoughts, how did it know where to grow? How did it decide which side of the wall to live in? Didn't it like Mrs Thompson's side? Maybe it wasn't a clever plant because otherwise, it would have chosen somewhere far better to live. There was a public park ten minutes' walk from Piety's house; it should have planted itself there, among the short grass so it would have the company of trees.

"Pi-Pi."

She picked up Tommy, settling him on her hip, squashing the too-fat nappy.

"Look at the little plant, Tommy-Tum."

He blinked at the marvel and turned his smile on her. To Piety, it seemed as if the sun had come out from behind a cloud.

"One day," she whispered, with her lips against his downy ear, "We will grow some flowers. And they will be beautiful."
"Boo-ful," her brother replied.
"We'll get a house together, and I will make us a garden." Her little brother beamed. "You'd like that wouldn't you, Tommy-Tum?"

She made a tickly spider hand on his bare belly. Tommy chuckled. After, they went and watched Jackanory before teatime.

In class the following day, Piety stuck her hand up high.

"Yes, Piety?"
"Oo, Miss. Do insects think?"

The class erupted into hysterics.

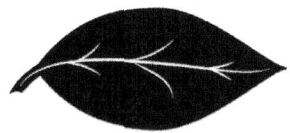

## Chapter Two

"What the fuck are you doing?" Piety's mother stood in the broken doorway of the bathroom. "Get those towels off you. Is that your dad's shirt?"

Mum held a round hairbrush in one hand and a can of hairspray in the other. On one side, her blonde flicks swept back stiff with spray; like the woman on the front of *Honey* magazine, the other side hung down a little fluffy. She was getting ready to go out for the night. Piety had only been dimly aware of the sound of the hairdryer stopping and was startled by Mum's arrival. The mustard-yellow towel over her shoulder slipped down to her elbow. She had been practicing her 'Tears of a Saint' pose.

Earlier in the week, the class had been taken to the school library to look at art books for a new project. Miss Sparrow had given them fifteen minutes to find something on Leonardo da Vinci, for a new project. Piety raced between the bookshelves – to the annoyance of the librarian, who constantly reprimanded everyone and said 'shh' a lot. Piety dragged the largest book she could find from a shelf. A large square hardback of paintings. Aaron

Brockley, the twins: Billy and Mike Hannigan, and Richard Burns huddled around a corner table giggling over nudes. Leonardo da Vinci was genuinely nice, but Piety had been drawn to the weirdly elongated figures by someone called El Greco.

At dinnertime, she returned to the library to sit with the Holy Virgin, sad-looking nobles, saints, and Jesus. She discovered *The Tears of Saint Peter* by El Greco. It portrayed the white-bearded saint against a dark tree or rock with two smaller figures in the distance. He looked like a sad, skinny Father Christmas. Peter clasped his hands and gazed heavenwards with an expression Piety couldn't determine. He looked like he was about to cry, his eyes twinkled with moisture. She felt a rush of compassion for him. *What did I do wrong?* He seemed to say. *I'm so sorry.* She wanted to tell him that everything would be all right. She had no words to express why she felt this way. Another picture showed the saint upside down on a cross. She didn't know why he was upside down and thought that only Jesus had been nailed to a cross. Peter wore a strange white thing that wasn't like Dad's undies. And here was another one, Saint Sebastian, but his underpants were smaller. Maybe Jesus did wear undies after all. But her favourite was still the El Greco picture. She lost track of time, and the librarian had to shoo her out. In the painting, Saint Peter wore a metallic-blue tunic with a golden-yellow shawl thing, and it was this pose she was attempting to emulate when her mother appeared.

"What's wrong with you? You need your head

feeling, Piety Scroggins. Now scoot," Mum said, pushing her out of the bathroom, hitching her turquoise mini up and knickers down before Piety turned away.

Dad was watching a film. One of those action ones he liked. It was black and white, which he didn't like so much. Piety leaned against the door frame and watched for a short while before going to sit on the back doorstep to look at the little green shoot. It had a leaf that hadn't been there two days ago.

"Pi! Get me a beer!" Dad shouted from his saggy armchair.
"What's for tea?" She handed the chilly, wet bottle over.
"Dunno, ask your mum." He didn't take his eyes off the screen.
"Muuuuum."
"For Christ's sake, Pi, can't you give us a break for one bloody minute?"
Mum was applying lipstick in the hall mirror. "Eddie. Eddie!" Dad made a noise of acknowledgement. "You ready yet? We're leavin' in a minute."

Dad peeled himself out of the chair. He patted Mum's bottom as he passed on the way upstairs. Dad always listened to the transistor radio when he was getting ready, she heard Dad singing along to *The Most Beautiful Girl in the World*. Not very well, she mused.

In the kitchen, she opened the fridge. An open packet of processed meat, the remains of a block of cheese with white stuff all over it, half a loaf of white sliced bread and a half bottle of milk. She picked Tommy up and sat him on the kitchen table. Poured a glass of milk and let him drink.

"What would you like for tea tonight, Tommy-Tum?"
"Badada!"
"Banana?"

She searched the cupboards. She looked in the fridge again. She hated to disappoint her brother. A smile suddenly appeared on her face. She spun around.

"This," she cupped her hands. "Is a magic banana!" He stared into her empty palms. "It's an invisible banana! Sh. Don't tell anyone." Tommy didn't seem convinced. "It's pretend. We can pretend whatever we want." She made an exaggerated thinking face; one forefinger to her lips. "Hm, what will I have for tea? I know, spaghetti and meatballs."
"Mee-baws."

Piety went through the motions of opening a tin of 'My Mum's spaghetti' and a tin of meatballs. She put her pretend pan on the cooker. Stirred. Placed two invisible plates on the table and served up. She sat Tommy on a chair and took the opposite one.

"How is your meal tonight, mister Scroggins?" She grinned, spun invisible spaghetti, and sucked. Her brother looked mournfully at the empty space before him. "Oops!" She wiped pretend sauce from her face. "It flicked my nose. I have sauce on my nose." The little boy smiled. "C'mon, eat up. Yummy, yummy."

Tommy joined in and soon the pair were giggling

and flicking invisible sauce about the kitchen. She told him that one of his meatballs had jumped off his plate and rolled beneath the cooker. Tommy made a startled 'o' with his mouth. "Maybe the kitchen pixies will have it for supper," she laughed. Her brother shrieked with delight.

"Keep the fuckin' noise down," Dad grumbled, plodding down the stairs.

Piety and Tommy shrank in their seats. She put her finger to her mouth, *sh*.
Dad was wearing his new blue suit with the widest flares and a big tie with flowers. Mum had on a new mini dress with a check pattern and puffy, white sleeves.

"You look smashing." Piety commented. Mum and Dad always looked great when they went out.
Mum did a fake curtsy, "Ta, chuck."
"Come on," Dad chivvied. "Or it'll be packed before we get there."
"Don't let anyone in. Do you hear me?" Mum warned Piety. "Don't answer the door to anyone, especially that nosy cow over the road. Right?"
"Yes, mum."
"We'll be back by half ten. No muckin' about."
She gave Tommy a kiss on the top of his head and left.

The door closed. The clack of Mum's heels faded up the street. Piety knew they wouldn't be home at ten-thirty. Sometimes they went to a club or would meet up with friends and go to their house for more drinks. On those nights, her little brother crawled into Piety's bed because he was scared. Piety was scared too, but she didn't let her little brother know. She would lie awake staring at the ceiling, waiting for the click of the door and the loud giggling and clumping sounds that marked her parents' stumbling return.

"Hungy, Pi-Pi."
Piety scooped him up and cuddled him. "I know, Tommy-Tum."

She made them a sandwich each with the remains of the bread and curled meat slices. There was no margarine, so it was dry and hard to swallow. They didn't want to watch the news or some costume drama, so they put *The Sweeney* on. Piety felt all grown up sitting in Mum's place while Tommy sat in Dad's saggy chair. Apart from the chomping and swallowing noises, they watched in silence. She knew that Jack Regan and George Carter were the good guys, but she wasn't sure about the rest. They kept talking about *poppies*, and a *fence* and *grass*, but none of these things ever showed up in the series. The best bit was the music, and afterwards, they sat side-by-side on the settee pretending to drive, belting out the theme tune.

"Do you want more milk?" she asked.
Her brother nodded. She poured the last of the milk into a glass. He drank it. They went to bed.

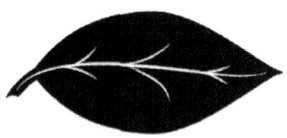

When Piety was two years old, she had been 'taken into care'. She didn't remember this time and did not know what it meant nor why it had happened. She only knew because she had once overheard Mum and Dad arguing.

"You want it to happen again?" Dad yelled.
"You could get off your bloody arse once in a while, I'm knackered!" Mum retorted, clutching her round belly. Piety couldn't remember what Mum looked like back then, sometimes Piety couldn't see her face at all because when she looked up at her, all she saw was a bump the size of a space hopper.
"You're a lazy cow, Ali."
"Oh. That's rich coming from you!"
"You're the one that gave her the bruises! That's why she was taken!"

The words 'taken into care' meant nothing. But she had been taken. Did this mean someone had stolen her? When she closed her eyes and tried to squeeze a memory or two out, all she saw was a vague figure with black hair. The smell of biscuits and flowers. Mum never baked and had blonde hair, and wore cheap perfume from the supermarket. Sometimes she wondered if it was a dream, or she had made it up, or seen it on television. Sometimes she got things muddled up and grownups got impatient with her; they sighed and rolled their eyes. She thought she had sat on someone's knee. She thought she had been hugged. She had been given a small cake and someone had said 'Happy Birthday, Piety'. The cake was small, pink and had one candle. The cake was real. Of this she was certain.

This was all before Tommy was born. Her little brother was four years younger and was the most beautiful child on earth. When she looked at her brother colouring with his fat crayon stumps, head bent, brows knitted in concentration, she was sure that he had been sent from Heaven. He looked to her like a cherub from one of the books in the school library; blonde waves fell past his ears and his eyes were the most startling blue. All he was missing was a pair of wings.

"Mum, can we make a cake?"
"What for?" Mum snapped. Piety shrugged. "I haven't got money to waste on stupid things like that. It's no one's birthday."

Piety poked her toe on the floor. Grey and red linoleum squares; the spaces in-between contained worlds of crust. Streaks of brown where chairs had been dragged back and forth. They'd had a cake when it was Tommy's fifth birthday three weeks ago; Mum bought it from *Kwik Save*. They'd gone to the local community centre, where Mum and Dad drank beer all afternoon and Piety and Tommy had been shown how to play darts by an old man who smelt of Old Spice and pork scratchings.
Sometimes, the local kids had their birthday parties here, but Mum had forgotten to organise anything.

"I'll buy one when it's your birthday. Okay?"
Piety's birthday wasn't until June.
"But I wanted to make one. A real one, with flour and eggs and —"
"For Christ's sake, Pi! Go and play in your room!" Mum shoved her away.

She slunk up the stairs, catching the sole of her sock on a splinter. She picked paint off a door frame. White. Green. Pink. Cream. Wood. It was as satisfying as picking a scab. Lifting a layer with the tip of her nail and uncovering the paint beneath. Someone must have painted the house before she lived here. She did not remember her dad doing any decorating. The wallpaper was hanging loose in the corner of her bedroom. Underneath was partially scraped-off cream paper with tiny blue flowers all over. She wondered who had lived here before her family. She wondered if they had children. Sometimes, she tried to picture the family that lived here before. Had they been happy?

"Would you like some help, Tommy?" She sat cross-legged next to him on the square of orange carpet — Dad had got it from someone at work. Something stuck to the back of her thigh. She peeled part of a beer bottle label away, screwed it up and tossed it across the room. She and Tommy coloured in silence for a while.
"Tommy-Tum. What do you want to be when you grow up?"
He stopped colouring in a jolly cartoon dog with a lolling tongue. He sat back and considered.
"Hm," he said. Screwed up his face so that his lips touched his nose, and breathed in deep. "A pilat. And a poleetman. And a feshional paghetti maker."
"A pilot? Do you like planes?"
"No. A pilate!"
"That's what a pilot is. They fly planes."
"Not planes. Chips."
Piety frowned. "Ships? Oh, a pirate!"
Tommy beamed and nodded.
Piety decided not to ask any more questions.

When Piety asked Carol Beverley what she wanted to be when she grows up, Carol said she thought she might like to be a nurse. She laughed when Piety said, mermaid.
"That's silly," Carol said. "You can't be a mermaid; they aren't really real. You have to be something real, like a nurse, or a secretary. Or a teacher." She added.
"Why do you want to be a nurse?"
"They look after people. And they wear nice uniforms. I like the little paper hats."
"Oh. I like mermaid tails."
"But you can't be a mermaid. Choose something real."
"Okay, a teacher. I think I'd be good at that."
"You have to be dead clever to be a teacher," Carol commented.
"I can be clever," Piety said. "I help our Tommy with stuff."
Carol made a sound between a sigh and a groan, "Hmm."

It didn't seem like her friend believed she could do it. So, she was going to work extra hard in lessons, and then she'd surprise everyone, including Carol Beverley.

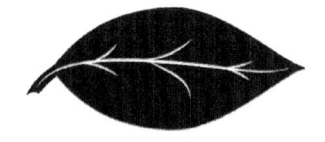

## Chapter Three

There was a knock at the front door.
"Pi!"
Piety clattered down the stairs, swung open the door, and froze.
"Who is it?"
"It's Miss Halifax."
"Can I come inside, Piety?" said Miss Halifax, she smiled.
"Who are you?" Mum came to the door. "What d'you want?"
"May I come in, Mrs Scroggins? I just wanted to have a chat."
"What about?"
Mum had one hand on the half-open door, her body blocking the way. She told Piety to go watch the telly, but Piety peeked around the living room door and listened.
"Mrs Scroggins, I'm Nerys Halifax, I'm the nurse at Piety's school."
"What's she done?"
"Oh, nothing. Nothing at all Mrs Scroggins. I only wanted to ask you a couple of questions, if that's okay."
The door was pulled closed a few inches. Piety couldn't see Miss Halifax, only the back of her

mum, hand on her hip; she had a ladder up the back of her tan tights and a Cornflake stuck to her mini skirt.
"Well, if she's not in trouble, there's nothing to ask."
"Has Piety got a GP?" the school nurse blurted.
"What?"
"For our records. I didn't see a family practitioner for her in my records."
"Wasn't that all done when she started school?"
"Well, I checked, and there seem to be a couple of blank sections. You do have a family GP, don't you Mrs Scroggins?"
"Nosy, aren't you?"
"Please, I'm just trying to get the correct information."
"Yes. We have."
"And can I ask the name of your GP?"
"Doctor Clarke."
"And when did Piety last see Doctor Clarke?"
Mum shrugged.
"It's… Piety has been having a few little accidents in school."
"All kids get bumps and knocks, that's just kids. What you sayin'?" Mum's voice sounded weird.
"No. I mean, she hasn't been having accidents as in falling and suchlike. She," the nurse's discomfort was evident by her tone. "Has *accidents*. You know, she goes to the toilet in class," her voice soft.
Mum's head turned. Piety shot back out of view. Shame spread through her, like a puddle of her wee under the desk. She went hot and shaky. She didn't hear what else was said. The door slammed and Mum exploded,

"I told you to watch your drinking. What in Christ's name is wrong with you?" Mum took hold of her

above one elbow and shook her, "Stop, drinking, so much."
"Ow, mum."
Mum's fingers pressed her flesh against the bone in a crab-like vice. "Why can't you be normal? I don't want anyone else coming to the door complaining about you. Do I make myself clear? Not school, not neighbours, no one."
"Ow."
Mum kept shaking her in a pincer grip, tossing Piety's hair about her face and rattling her teeth. "It's always one thing or another with you. Why can't you be more like your brother? You got no bloody sense. Just behave from now on. Understand? I said, *do you understand?"* Mum was scarlet, bug-eyed, and scary. She pulled Piety up onto her toes until their faces were close. "And stop pissing in class."

She gave Piety a rough shove. Piety toppled back, caught her heel on the bottom step of the stairs and fell, clunking her head on the newel post on the way.

"If anyone else comes to the door 'cos of you, I'll fuckin' slap you all round the backyard!" Mum stormed off. Piety raced upstairs.

Mum was what other people described as petite. She wasn't much taller than Piety, with slim arms and legs, a little waist and a 'tight round arse', as Dad called it. But she was mighty strong for her size. Piety rubbed her upper arm where the sensation remained.

From her bedroom window, she watched Miss

Halifax trying to drag the front gate shut. It was wonky and scraped across the tarmac; unless you used both hands and lifted it. But the school nurse didn't know to do that. Piety wanted to call out the window, but it had been jammed shut for ages. Miss Halifax glanced up and saw her watching. Piety thought that Miss Halifax looked like Saint Peter in the painting. It made her sad for the nurse. She felt horrible for making Mum explode. She must try harder.

She went to check on her little plant in the wall. She thought of it as hers because, well, she was the only person who looked out for it. She didn't have to water it; the rain did that. But she did talk to it sometimes, encouraging it to uncurl its leaves. This day was a bright sunshiny day, and the light made the leaves luminous.

"Gorgeous," she whispered.

It had four leaves now. They seemed fragile as the tissue paper that Miss Sparrow kept in one of the craft trays, and shone like gems.
"Look Tommy, another leaf."

Tommy wasn't interested in the plant. He was busy turning the remaining fat pedal on an upside-down tricycle. He found a stick and started jabbing at the mound of slimy carpets. His nappy was fat as usual and smeared with green algae. She wondered if she should find a pot to put the seedling in. It would need soil; she could go to the park and easily scoop some up. Or she could take it to the park and replant it there. But she didn't want to do that. It was hers. She wanted to be able to see it every day. To watch it grow bit by bit. To discover what it was going to become. Would it turn into a flower or a tree? She had never seen a seedling before. She rummaged about the kitchen cupboards looking for a suitable empty container, one that Mum wouldn't miss. The right shape and size. They used yoghurt pots in school sometimes for painting, but her family did not eat yoghurt.

Through the window, she saw the top of Tommy's head. He had somehow climbed over the stack of broken things and up the horrible carpet mound. Piety waved. Tommy waved back. Tommy disappeared. And screamed.
Piety dashed outside. Slipped on the damp stone and fell hard onto her side. It hurt, but that didn't matter. Tommy was lying on his front screaming, face almost purple.
"Mum! Mum!" she yelled.
When Piety tried to pick him up, he screamed louder. She didn't know what to do. Crying and snotty and slipping on the slimy flagstones, gravel and grit stabbing her feet, she careened into the house.
"Mum! Mum!"
"Oh, my god. Can't I have a minute's peace?" Mum shouted.
"Tommy's hurt mum. He fell."
"Shit!"
Mum bounded through the house, slippers flapping. Shrieked when she caught her foot on the upturned trike. Swore at the "friggin' mess out here". Bundled Tommy into her arms, where he screamed louder.
"Baby, baby, what's happened, tell mummy."
"He fell. He fell off the carpets."
She followed Mum indoors.

"What was he doing up there? Why weren't you watching him?"

Piety couldn't tell her mum she was looking for a pot. She couldn't tell her about the tiny plant growing in the wall against all the odds. She couldn't tell her mum that she was paying more attention to *it* than her brother.
"I was," she mumbled.
But Mum didn't hear because of Tommy's cries.
"I'll have to take him to the A and E. Shh, it's okay."
"What's the A and E, mum?"
But Mum was using the telephone.
"Yeah, hi. Shh. I need a taxi. Now...sixteen Kirk Road. Ta. The A n E Fazakerley. Yeah. Ta."
"What's happening, mum?"
"Taking him to hospital. Shh. shh. Just go away!"
"Don't bounce him, mum. It hurts him." Piety couldn't stop the tears from pouring like she was plugged into her little brother's pain.
"Shh, shh. It's okay, baby."
"He's crying more. Can't you make him stop?" She bunched her fists in front of her mouth. Tommy was shrieking horribly.
"I know what I'm doing!"
"He's really red, Mum,"
"Shh. Shh." Bounce bounce.
"Mum. He's really red."
"Shut up, Piety!"
"But you're hurting him."
"Don't you dare!" Mum glared.
Her eyes were like two huge glass ollies; looked like they might pop right out of her head. She was angrier than when Nurse Halifax had knocked and told about her weeing in class. Angrier than when Piety had accidentally got stuck in the washing

machine. Piety cringed from the incandescence of Mum's scowl and fell silent. A car horn beeped outside, and Mum clambered into the taxi clutching Tommy. When Piety followed, she snapped, "You stay here!" and off they went.

She stood on the pavement and watched until the taxi turned the corner. Over the road, Mrs Lawler turned back to sweeping her doorstep.

It was all her fault; Piety knew this. Mum and Dad said so.

"What were you thinking? You stupid little girl."
"She doesn't think."
"What were you doing?"
"Not minding him."
"How many times…"
"Selfish. Fuckin selfish."
"He could have a permanent bend in his arm 'cause of you!"
"You spend too much time daydreaming!"
"And we had that woman from the school."
"Bloody stupid."
"Go to your room!"

Dad cuffed the back of her head as she went to bed without any tea. But she didn't mind that so much if it meant getting away from the disappointed glares of her parents. Tommy was asleep on his back. He wore only pyjama bottoms because they couldn't fit his top over the plaster cast. He lay with his knees slightly bent, fallen outwards, arms on the pillow either side of his head; like he was a surrendering soldier. His fair curls were a ruffled mass with strands stuck to dried tears. Puffy cheeks pink-tinged. Piety knelt at his bedside and whispered,

"I'm sorry, Tommy-Tum. I honestly am." Then, "Dear God, please make Tommy better. And don't let his arm be forever bent. I didn't mean it, honest I didn't. Sometimes I can't remember what I'm supposed to be doing. Sometimes there's such a lot to remember, and I know you have a lot too, like all the animals, and people and making things grow and, stuff. I will be a good girl from now on. I promise. Make it so he's okay. And happy. Happy most of all."

With that, she gave his sweaty forehead a little kiss and got into her bed. Pulled the sheet and blanket up around her ears, and silently cried herself to sleep.

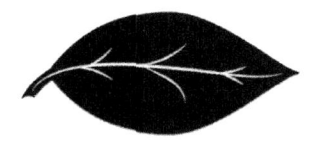

Piety didn't much like Mrs Lawler. Mrs Lawler lived in the house diagonally opposite. Sometimes she could see her peeking around her curtains. Whenever Piety was playing in the street and Mrs Lawler got into her car, she would look at Piety a certain way. Piety thought that Mrs Lawler might be a teacher; not in her school because she wouldn't need to drive to it, and, she hadn't seen her there, but because she had that look that teachers sometimes get; *What are you doing Aaron Brockley? What have you got under the desk?* Mrs Lawler looked at her like that.

Sometimes Piety felt like sticking her tongue out but never did because that would be rude. In Sunday School, they talked about being good, and polite, and honouring thy father and thy mother – but she didn't know how to do the last one.

"Nosy biddy." Her mum would say. "Hasn't got a life of her own so she sticks her nose in other people's business." Sometimes Mum called Mrs Lawler a 'fucking nosy biddy' or 'bitch face' or 'snitch'. Piety had no idea what caused the enmity between her mum and the neighbour across the road. It puzzled her that Mum felt that way. Sometimes, when she knew there was no one around and she was playing, she would mutter to her doll, "Fucking nosy biddy." It felt thrilling but naughty to say, and she would clamp her lips tight afterwards.

Once, when Piety had been quite small; Tommy was only a baby and couldn't play out on the road, Mrs. Lawler had spoken to Piety. She actually crossed the road to come and talk!
"That's a nice doll."

Piety stood stock still, head down, focused on the spindly, naked toy with the horribly hacked blonde hair and fingers that bore the marks of Tommy's first teeth.

"How is your mum? And the new baby?"
Piety shrugged.
"If she needs any help, she can ask."
Nod.
"Does your dolly have a name?"
Shrug.

"Does your new baby have a name?"
"Tommy."
"That's a lovely name, short for Thomas, isn't it?"

Piety looked at Mrs Lawler without moving her head. Mrs. Lawler had quite a large nose, it was the first thing she saw as she glanced from beneath her long fringe. Maybe that's why she was nosy. A bang on the window made Piety and Mrs Lawler jump.

"Get in!" She heard Mum's voice through the glass, her face tight with anger.

Piety didn't see what Mrs Lawler looked like because she was busy hurrying through the door. But she left her doll on the wall. She watched Mrs Lawler cross the road and go into her own house, she looked at the skinny doll. When she opened the front door again, Mum shouted,

"Shut the door! Don't think you're going out there again for that nosy bitch to get her claws in you. What did she say?"
"Nothing."

Mum tutted and slouched off to the kitchen for a cigarette. Piety didn't like that her mum smoked, but she would never say that to Mum. The house always smelt of smoke, and Mum's two fingers on her right hand had yellow patches.

Piety pulled back the net curtain, so that it was like a veil against her head and shoulders, and looked at her doll lying on the wall; one arm sticking up in the air, one leg thrust forward as though leaping.

When the first spot of rain darkened the paintwork, she asked Mum if she could fetch her doll.

"You've got other toys," was the curt reply.

Piety didn't argue. She knew that there was never any point in arguing with Mum; that'd get you a 'good hiding'.

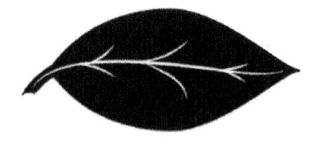

## Chapter Four

Summer arrived. Although the beginning of June was cold and frosty, like wintertime, it soon heated up and got hotter and hotter as it bled into July. Piety and Tommy, along with all the other kids on the street; and the neighbouring streets, spent most of their waking hours out-of-doors. Never-ending days outside, they lived on the street and home was only a place you went to eat and sleep. Space to race and stretch your limbs and yell your head off like a pack of unowned dogs howling at the hot sun. Mum would not allow kids in the house, so Piety's birthday was a miscellaneous troop of children taking jellies in bright paper pots from the front wall — she didn't get the promised cake.

Dad would sit on neighbour's walls, chatting with the men, and sometimes she heard them whistle when women walked past. *I'm Not in Love* by 10CC and *Give a Little Love* by the Bay City Rollers blared through open windows and cars, and the kids would dance madly until they got too hot and fell panting to the ground gasping until the ice cream van came. Mum sat in the backyard with her friend Julie, flicking through magazines, drinking, smoking, and slagging off women Piety didn't know.

Kirk Road bloomed with chalk drawings, hopscotch squares, and sweet and iced lolly wrappers. Sometimes, the other kids told Piety she couldn't join their games or told her to go away, because she played wrong, they said. She didn't remember the rules of clapping rhymes or British Bulldog. She always got tangled in the rope, so couldn't join skipping games, and was never able to catch jacks on the back of her hand. *You're rubbish, Pi. You're clumsy. You'll only spoil the game.* When they played hide-and-seek, she was always found first because she didn't know where best to hide. So, she leaned with her back against the low wall and watched, laughing when they laughed and clapping when one of them successfully caught the ball. Mum did let her have a pair of her old tights; after she nagged so much, that she dropped a tennis ball inside so she could whip it side to side against a wall like the other girls. But she wasn't good at that either.

One day, she tagged along behind a gang of kids who were playing knock-and-run. This entailed sneaking up to someone's front door, hammering loudly and waiting until the last tingly minute before running away, and hiding somewhere close enough to watch the bemused expression on the faces of the people who opened their doors. Sometimes, the person would shout and wave their fist, and all the kids would hunker down giggling. Piety followed the bunch to the end of the road. They stopped outside the big old house on the corner. The witch's house.

One of the older boys, Ian, pointed at it. "This one. I

dare ye."
A smaller boy, Archie, looked at the house with round eyes. "Here?"

The rest made chicken noises until Archie stuck his chin out and shushed them all. He crept up the front path and knocked on the glass side panel. From the gate, Piety could see a dark shape moving slowly to the door. Archie ran. Everyone scattered. Some raced back down Kirk Road, and a couple leapt into the neighbour's garden, peeking over the fence. Piety stood there, frozen with indecision, and watched the front door open. A face blinked out, cautious at first before opening the door wider. She saw an old woman with a face like a chewed caramel toffee, the ones in Mum's Christmas chocolate box that no one liked except Piety. She wobbled down the path a short way.

"What do you want?"

Her voice sounded like the old trees in her garden might sound like if they could talk. She wore a blue apron over a brown skirt and a brown cardigan. She didn't look scary at all this close. Piety shook her head and looked left and right for the other kids. The old lady followed her gaze.

"You live down Kirk Road, don't you?"

Piety nodded. How did she know that? Was she going to tell her parents that she had played knock-and-run? She became scared. Mum would throw a fit.

"I'm sorry." Piety's voice came out small and

squeaky.
"Don't worry, I won't tell," the old lady seemed to read her mind. "Do you want an apple? You look like you could do with feeding up," she indicated the gnarled trees. Piety saw the clusters of little red globes hanging there. She nodded but didn't move. "Well go on, it won't pick itself," the old woman gestured with a little yellow hand.

Piety moved slowly, watching the old woman all the time as she headed into the uncut grass. She tugged free the nearest fruit and clutched the blood-red apple to her chest.

"Now go on, be off with you."
"Thank you," Piety said. "Thank you!"

She dashed from the garden and up Kirk Road, running and grinning like a mad puppy dog, until she reached her house. The other kids were impressed for a short while until Ian said, authoritatively, that witches recognised other witches and she was abandoned. Mrs Thompson, the next-door neighbour, was out sweeping her front step, a lot of the old women did this *and* washed their front windows. Why they did this was beyond Piety, didn't the rain do that?

"Take no notice of them, love." Mrs Thompson spoke as she swept.
She stopped and leant on the broom handle. Piety thought she might ask where she got the apple from.
"I didn't steal it." She said, holding the red fruit out. Mrs Thompson just gave a little smile. "I see your plant is growing well."

Plant? What did she mean? She remembered the straggly thing. Could she see into their backyard from her bedroom window? Piety supposed she must be able to, seeing as she could see into Mrs Thompson's. Hers was all potted flowers and baskets trailing pink, purple and yellow from hangers like gaudy waterfalls. Mrs Thompson came a little closer.

"I think it's wonderful that you're interested in plants. Do you know what it is?" Piety shook her head. "It's a Buddleia, a butterfly bush. Except yours isn't quite a bush yet is it, love?"
"Bud-lee-a," Piety repeated. "Is it 'cause it likes butterflies?"
"Butterflies like *it*," her neighbour said. "I know it's a little weedy now, but just wait until it grows bigger. It'll be a beauty. Did you see the purple spire last year?"

Purple spire? Churches had spires, did plants too? She recalled the elongated flower that had sprouted on the tip. That must be what the old woman means.

Mrs Tompson went on, "The beauty of the butterfly bush is that it is extremely resilient to bad conditions. It can put up with all sorts of mistreatment, and neglect. It thrives in the most unlikely conditions and grows in the most remarkable places, like on the sides of abandoned buildings high up, and in gutters. A tenacious little thing."

And then she went inside. Piety took a bite of the red apple thinking about how a beautiful tree could grow from an abandoned building.

She was allowed to go to the public library during the summer holidays. Allowed wasn't quite right, her parents didn't keep an eye on her movements throughout the summer once she was out the front door. No one bothered, kids were like pet dogs put outside in the morning to roam the streets singly or in packs. Even Tommy at five years of age played out until all hours, coming home only to eat, sleep and watch TV. It was a half-hour walk, past school and the park. Sometimes she took her brother, but mostly she went by herself. She liked the library, it was cool inside and made her feel all calm and restful, but she couldn't stop laughing when she read something that tickled her, and once she whooped so loudly that one of the librarians told her to leave. Afterwards, she sat on a swing in the park and watched some kids from school playing on the witch's hat. Aaron Brockley was at the very top, wearing a Liverpool tee-shirt with a big number eight on the back, yelling at the top of his lungs as the hat spun round and round and rocked back and forth. Piety knew she was too clumsy to have a go, besides, she heard Aaron proclaiming to everyone who could hear, that they shouldn't go on *that* swing, because "Pee Pee Scroggy has done a wee on it!"

And then it was over and back to school. Everyone had new shoes, new uniforms, new satchels, and new haircuts. But not Piety. Mum said they couldn't afford it. Dad wasn't getting the work like he used to.

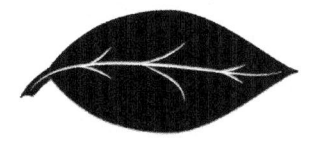

Piety knew it was November because they'd had Halloween — she and Tommy stayed up late to watch an old black-and-white horror film, which gave her nightmares. And they'd had Bonfire Night. Some of the men and bigger boys in the street had made a massively huge bonfire on the wasteland opposite the houses. There had been fireworks and someone gave her a sparkler and she ran around drawing letters and circles in the air until it fizzed into blackness. And later a fire engine arrived and put the bonfire out, so the grown-ups went to the pub.

All the children were gathered in the big hall for a special assembly after lunch. They sat on the floor cross-legged in rows, with the teachers sitting primly on chairs around the perimeter. A TV was rolled in on a high trolley and positioned in front of the stage. Mr Bleasedale had brought in his home video recorder. It took some time to set it up and most of the kids got bored and chatted. Piety watched the proceedings with interest. There were lots of wires and the fat metal end was pushed into more than one socket before the screen cleared and she could see a view of lots of people standing in straight lines, like blocks of toy soldiers. Mr Bleasedale clapped his hands, and everyone stopped talking and faced the front.

"Righty-o." said the headmaster, "Does anyone

know what day it was yesterday?"
Some of the kids made 'oo-oo' sounds as they thrust their arms up. Piety put her hand up too; it was Sunday yesterday, wasn't it? Sometimes she got the days of the week mixed up.
"Yes, Piety?" He appeared happy that so many children knew what day of the week it was.
"It was Sunday, Mr Bleasedale." Someone along her row sniggered.
"Yes, it was." He smiled. "And do we know what was special about it?"

Piety thought and thought. What happened yesterday? Could Mr Bleasedale know she had broken a mug when she was doing the dishes? Did he know she had peeled the wallpaper off behind the wonky wardrobe in the bedroom? Had Mrs Lawler telephoned the school and told them that Piety Scroggins was a horrible sister and that she had let her little brother cross the road without looking? She felt herself shrink as eyes turned to her.

"It was Remembrance Sunday!" a boy shouted from the back.
"Yes, it was, Luke," Mr Bleasedale said. "I'm very happy you knew, but shall we not shout out in future?"

Piety couldn't hear what Mr Bleasedale was talking about now. Her ears were filled with that weird *whoom-whoom-whoom* noise that sometimes happened when she had answered a question wrong, or when she felt dizzy because she had not had anything to eat for a while. An elbow nudged her. Carol Beverley was one of the few children in

Beacon Park Primary School that did not make fun of Piety, and whom she regarded as a friend. Carol pointed at the TV. Piety's ears cooled, she could hear a woman announcer talking about the army, and the navy, and something about sacrifice. There was row upon row of people walking forwards and saluting to a tall stone.

"The Queen!" a girl shouted as Her Majesty appeared on the screen. An appreciative murmur went up.

*"...Her Majesty the Queen lays her wreath of poppies at the foot of the Cenotaph..."* said the voice from the TV.

"Ahh, doesn't she look lovely?" simpered Carol Beverley. Carol was always talking about the royal family and the clothes they wore. Piety couldn't see the attraction. Dad said they were scroungers. Dad said the royal family was a "friggin waste of space". Dad didn't like the royal family.

On the TV screen, bands played music. The children were encouraged to sing along; Mr Bleasedale was ridiculously pink as he belted out the words. The announcer named each tune. She heard her say "And now, *The Minstrel Boy* by Thomas Moore, for the Irish regiments." Something about the tune made Piety's chest swell, she didn't know why. Words appeared on the pull-down screen above the stage,

*The Minstrel Boy to the War is gone*
*In the ranks of death you will find him*

She mumbled only the first two lines before her emotions overwhelmed her. Her breath heaved into her mouth like a huge ball of cotton. She did not know why she felt this way. She didn't understand why it felt as though she had a rolling wave in her chest. Her head went all hot. Fat water drops soaked her grey school skirt. A snot bubble formed in one nostril. She pressed her lips tight for fear she would bawl aloud, and everyone would stare and laugh — *Piety Scroggins is thick, thick, thick!* A hand firmly grasped her upper arm. She was hoisted to her feet, led from the hall, hurried down the corridor and into a classroom. A paper tissue presented itself. She blew her nose and wiped her eyes on the sleeve of her cardigan.

"Feeling better?"

Piety looked at the knees facing her. Tan tights with a thick checked woollen skirt hugging them. She nodded. She continued staring at the floor as Miss Sparrow moved behind the desk, rummaged about in a drawer and a carrier bag.

"Here you go. This'll cheer you up." Piety took the chocolate wrapped in deep red plastic and shiny foil. She sucked it slowly until it split open, and a creamy caramel coated her tongue. "Now what was that all about?" asked Miss Sparrow. Piety shrugged. "Was your granddad in the war?"

Piety shrugged again. She had only met her grandparents once, briefly. She could barely recall what they looked like. She didn't know what war Miss Sparrow was talking about. Grandad had smelt strongly of aftershave and her grandmother hardly spoke to her.

"We will be doing our topic this week on the Second World War; will you be okay?"

Piety nodded. It hadn't been the mention of the war. Or the rows of military people. Or the solemnity which presented itself on the big TV screen. It was the music which had stirred her deepest emotions. The music had touched something deep down inside her. She couldn't even begin to describe to herself, how the music insinuated itself into her skin, her heart, her soul. Not all of it, that tune in particular. And a boy had died. She began bubbling and sobbing again.

"There, there. It's all fine now."

Suddenly, she did something that shocked Piety into silent immobility. Miss Sparrow hugged her. Never. Never before had a teacher hugged her. Never had she seen a teacher hug a child. Never had she been hugged by her parents. But someone had once, a long time ago. She broke into a new wave of blubbing. Her shoulders heaving as she bawled into her teacher's warm sweater. It felt wonderful. It was all the love in the world in a human blanket wrapped around tight and snuggly and it smelt of soap and chalk and something sweet and pretty. A sliver of memory popped into her head. It was a long time ago; she was crying, and a large woman was hugging her in a warm embrace that enveloped the whole of her. This felt the same. And she couldn't stop crying. Her tummy kept filling up with sadness and pushing up through her chest and pushing tears out of her eyes. She gurgled and twitched. Miss Sparrow held her at arm's length.

"Piety. You have to stop now."
"I... hic...can't...hic...
"You're getting hysterical, love!" Piety heard her say, "Shit," under her breath.

She was taken to the nurse's office. Miss Sparrow practically dragged her along the corridors, hurrying as fast as she could without running.

"Mrs Halifax. Nerys. Can you keep an eye on Piety? She got upset in assembly. I have to get back for the class." Miss Sparrow's voice was all high and wobbly.

Nurse Halifax cleaned Piety's face with a damp flannel. Called her a sensitive soul. She removed Piety's cardigan and let her lie on the bed of green plastic and drew a thin blue cover over her. She pulled a little curtain around for privacy and stroked her cheek before going to sit back behind her desk.

It was dark when Piety awoke, apart from a little glow through the curtain. She hopped down off the bed and pulled the curtain back. A lamp craned towards the wooden surface of the desk. The chair, with its permanent blue cardigan draped over it, was pushed in. Paperwork was stacked neatly in one corner. The door stood slightly ajar. The clock on the wall showed four o'clock.

She was late! She guessed that she must have slept all afternoon. Everyone will have gone home. She shuffled from the office with the blanket trailing behind. Beyond the nurse's room was a small seating area which opened onto the Teacher's Corridor — they called it this because the staffroom was at the other end, and at least one teacher could always be found there at any time. The caretaker was mopping the floor halfway along. About to ask Mr Bryan where Nurse Halifax was, a door opened to her right.

"Ah. Piety!"

Mr Bleasedale offered to take the blanket from her. Folding it, he asked if she felt better. Had she slept well? Piety nodded mutely. Nurse Halifax, he explained, had to go home, her baby was waiting for her. This was a revelation to Piety. She never thought about the school nurse, or teachers, having children of their own. She wondered if Mr Bleasedale had children. Did Miss Sparrow?
"Is it a boy or a girl?" She asked.
"A little boy. David," he said. Piety managed a smile. "You live on Kirk Road, don't you? Not far, ten, fifteen minutes?" Piety nodded. "I tried to call your parents," Piety froze, "But no one was answering."
"My dad's at work," she mumbled.
"I wondered if someone would come and collect you, under the circumstances." She stared, uncomprehending, at Mr Bleasedale. "Because you were upset, Piety."
She didn't understand why she would need her parents to walk her home. Piety had walked herself to and from school since she was six.
She shook her head, "I'm fine, Mr Bleasedale. Thank you. I'll be going now."
Mr Bleasedale gave her a quizzical look. Tipped his

head to one side as she departed.

On arriving back at her house, something caught her eye. Behind the front wall, she saw a white plastic carrier bag. The handles were tied together with old string and there was a piece of paper with writing sellotaped to it — *for the little girl*. Inside was a little troll doll with purple hair sticking up. She scrunched the package up small and went in, holding it behind her back.

Mum didn't notice, she simply said, "You're late," before telling her there was a Cup-a-Soup and a glass of milk in the kitchen.
"Where's Dad?"
"Out."

Piety ate in hers and Tommy's bedroom, she didn't want to watch the quiz show her mum was watching. She took the troll toy out of the plastic bag. It wasn't new, but it was clean, and someone had made a tiny dress for it. Who on earth could have left it there?

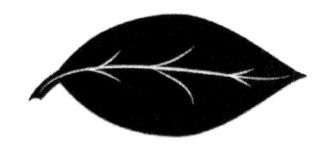

## Chapter Five

It was a rare visit to Grandma's house. Grandma and Grandad lived a bus ride away. Piety could not remember visiting before, but Mum said that she had been when she was little. She stared out of the window at the shops and derelict houses and huge patches of open land covered in rubble and kids chucking stones. She was wearing her best dress, the pretty floral one with the Peter Pan collar and deep border in yellow. It had been a seventh birthday present. It pinched under the arms and was tight across her stomach. It was too short in fact, and stuck out at the front like stiff paper. She wore a fluffy cardigan over it and was warm enough on the bus. Tommy sat next to her wearing a kind of all-in-one romper suit. Mum had cut the feet off to fit him, so he wore his red Wellington boots to hide the gap.

Mum and Dad sat together on the side-facing seat in front of them not talking. Mum wore her powder blue mini and the pink fitted sweater. Dad hadn't dressed up, not properly. He was wearing a tie though. At home, they had argued.

"Don't see why, just to visit that old bat."
"She'll expect it, Eddie. Y'know what she's like. Anyway, we need to make a good impression."

They had to walk quite a bit after getting off the bus. Thankfully, it wasn't too cold for December, but Piety felt the breeze through the knitted layer. Mum held Tommy's hand and kept tugging him along when he dawdled. He had to skip and do those little runs he did to keep up with Mum. Piety gripped Dad's hand tight, she didn't like the grey houses. Some had metal covers over the doors and windows. There were little front gardens, not like her road, but a lot of them weren't cared for. She didn't like the way Mum and Dad weren't talking. She didn't like that they were walking too fast.

Grandma and Grandad's house was second from the end. The garden was neat, the lawn cropped so short she could see the soil. Small shrubs were placed equidistant from each other and a yellow shrub at each corner had been shaped into thin pyramids. The front door was black and had a semi-circular window near the top, but she didn't think anyone could see out of it because it was made of that funny dimpled glass. Dad used the polished knocker. The neighbour's curtain was pulled to one side.

"What?" Dad jutted his chin.

When the door opened, Piety almost gasped with the heat that erupted from the little hallway.

"Hiya, Dad," said Mum.
"Y'all right, Frank?" said Dad.

"All right." Grandad stood to one side, and they all squeezed past. "Your mam's in the back." He smiled weakly at Piety and Tommy.

They all trooped through to the back room. Grandma had the telly on and didn't look up when they came in. She sniffed and held up her hand, the way the queen did when she waved. Piety watched two ladies in a cottage kitchen, one took something from an oven and put it on the table, "And there it is," she smiled. Piety couldn't tell what *it* was. Something pink and creamy with twirly blobs of cream decorating the top. The title music began to play, and the credits rolled.

Grandma waved them all in. "Sit, sit. Turn that down would you, Francis." Grandad dutifully turned the volume dial. "I never miss *Farmhouse Kitchen*," she sniffed as she looked them over.

"That's a short skirt, Alison."
Piety turned her head to see Mum's cheeks turn really pink.
"They're all the rage, mum."
"Not sure I like the jumper either." Mum chewed her bottom lip. "I expect you'll want a cuppa," Grandma told Grandad to make tea. In the blue pot, not the brown one. And the mugs. *Not* the best cups. She regarded the children.

"That didn't take long, did it?" she seemed to scrutinise Tommy.
"He's five years old, Sheila. Piety's nine. You'd know that if you bothered to visit." Dad sounded upset.
"Ed, no." Mum touched his knee lightly.

Grandma kept staring at Tommy. Piety looked at her brother. He swung his wellington booted feet, *thump, thump, thump* against the base of the settee and sniffed up a yellow dribble and regarded the older woman.

"How owd are you?" he asked.
"Cheeky little bugger, isn't he? I suppose you'll be wanting a biscuit?"
Tommy nodded. "Come with me then." She held out her hand, which he took smiling, and led him into the kitchen.
"Y'alright, our Alison?" Grandad hovered over the two-seater settee before finally settling down.
"Ali, it's Ali, Dad. Yeah, not bad."
Grandad nodded. "Good, good. And you, Eddie? Everything going okay? Found a job yet?"
"I do alright, Frank. Make ends meet. Y'know how it is at the mo."
"Aye, aye. But there's jobs ain't there, y'know? Plenty of options?"
"There is Frank, always plenty of options." Piety saw Dad give Mum a wink.
"And how is this young lady?" Grandad turned his attention to Piety.

Before she could answer, Tommy and Grandma returned. She carried a tray with cups and a small plate of biscuits.

"Move that paper, Francis. No, don't dump it there, put it on the sideboard."

She placed the tea tray on the low table in the middle of the room. Tommy came and squeezed himself between Piety and Mum. He was quiet. He shook his head when the biscuit plate was passed around. Piety saw his cheeks looked hot and fat. And he had his head tucked down so he got a double chin. He only ever looked like this when he had been told off. But Grandma hadn't told him off, she would have heard her.

Grandma took her tea. She had a dainty cup and saucer with pink flowers round the edge. "I hear Milly Randle's girl works at St. Marks." Grandma sipped her tea daintily. "You remember her, don't you? Jackie, isn't it? Well, she passed her teaching qualifications. Decent pay, Milly says. She always was a bright girl that one. And Susan Parker is the manageress at Kwik Save, looks dead smart in her suit. Oh, and I saw that lad you used to date before Edward, what was his name, Liam? Ian? Anyway, he's a copper. Can you believe that?"
"Alright, Mum, I get the point." Piety's mum held her mug, untouched in her lap.
"Point, love?"
Grandma had awfully piercing blue eyes. Piety found it hard to keep looking her in the face. Grandad looked at his shoes.

"Yeah, they all did good and got good jobs --"
"What? You mean, you didn't? Oh no, because you shacked up with this one here and haven't done a tap since you pushed that one out," she indicated Piety with a quick head tip.

Piety felt her face go fat and red like Tommy's.

"Y'know what? Forget it. Come on, we're going home."

"You haven't asked for what you came for, Alison. You haven't told us what you're after. Like you always do."
"Just leave it, Mum. We're going. We won't come again, okay?"
"I bet you will though. As soon as the dole's spent, you'll come crawling here for handouts. Like always, Alison."
"I don't!" Tommy flinched and clung onto Piety. "And it's Ali, not Alison. You know I hate Alison." Piety shrank back into the big settee. Mum, Dad, and Grandma were all standing up around the coffee table. "Ali. It's not hard to remember."
"As in ally cat," Grandma said.
"Sheila," Grandad gasped.
"Aye, aye," Dad put his arm around Mum. "We'll have less of that. She's your daughter. Have some respect."
"Respect? Respect?" Grandma's voice went higher. "When did she ever show me respect? Hey? Truanting. Smoking. Drinking. Putting it about. Shame. That's all she's ever given me. Shame. Pregnant at sixteen!" Grandma's face was all hard lines and white tightness. Piety slid off the settee clutching her brother and skirted behind her parents and into the hall.
"And you." Grandma raised her chin higher. "Call yourself a man? Giro man more like. Never knew such a pair of workshy dodgers in all me life."
"There is nothin', Sheila." Dad almost shouted. "Have you looked outside recently? There's loads of union blokes out rallying for work."
"Yeah, and if a job fell into *your* lap, Eddie Scroggins, it'd not be made welcome, would it? Was the other one an accident too? Eh?"
"Why can't you —"

"What, Alison? Why can't I what?"
"Just, stop," Mum's voice trailed off.

She looked like she was about to cry. Piety wanted everyone to stop arguing. To be friends. She wanted to go home. Tommy pushed his face into her stomach, and she wrapped her arms around his head.

"What, you want me to say, *there, there*, Alison, here's something to tide you over? Have a new coat, Alison? In fact, why don't I buy coats for all your family? *Your* family, Alison. *Yours*. Don't you remember what you said? They're mine, not yours and never will be. You made your bed, young lady, so bloody well lie in it."
"Oh. Get lost!"

Mum shrugged Dad off and stormed to the front door. Dad said something that Piety didn't hear, and Grandad came into the hallway to see them off. Mum was at the gate before Dad, Piety and Tommy had stepped outside.

"I'm sorry, Eddie. Here. No. It's fine, honestly," he pressed two tenners into Dad's hand. "Get the kiddies something will you?" Grandad gave Piety a sad smile.

The door closed gently behind them.

"Fuckin' cow," Dad said, ripping off his tie.
"Puckin' cow," Tommy said, quiet, but Piety heard.

Everyone was silent all the way home. It was horrible. Piety needed a wee and kept jiggling on the seat. Mum glared daggers at her. Tommy ran straight upstairs when they got home. Mum and Dad started shouting in the kitchen. Piety raced to the bathroom for the wee she'd been desperately holding onto. A door slammed shut downstairs. In the bathroom, she heard sobbing coming from the bedroom.

"What's up, mate?" She pushed the door shut behind her. He shook his head. "C'mon, you can tell me. Are you hungry?" Shake, shake. "Have you hurt yourself?" *No.* "Have you lost something?" He always got upset when he lost a favourite toy. *No.* She stroked his back, "Tommy-Tum, what's up?"
"Can't tell."
"Why?"
"'Cos."
"'Cos what?"
"Angma said."
Piety frowned. "Grandma said what?"
"Can't tell."
This went on for ages. Piety didn't know what to do. But when she said she was going to get Mum, he sat up quickly.
"No. Don't."
He looked scared. "Tommy, I'm really, really worried now. Please tell me."
"Sec-et."
"Okay. What secret? I can keep secrets; you know I can."
"You can't tell. Pomise." Piety promised. "Angma said she was going to cut my feet off 'cause I kicked her chair. She said Mum and Dad didn't weally want me, I was a accident like you, and I was naughty and ugry, and you're ugry too, and if I told anyone she would hurt me good and popper."

Piety's mouth dropped open. Tommy started crying again. Piety started crying when he showed her the tiny bruises at the top of his arm where Grandma had pinched him.

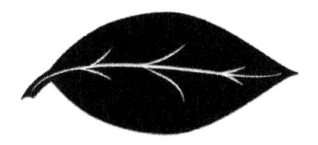

Wednesday twenty-second of December. The last day of school before the holidays. Piety rose early. Washed her hands and face in the bathroom sink. Combed her hair, and from the drawer in her bedside locker; amidst the plastic toys from cereal packets and creased playing cards, a torch in the shape of a pink pony and other items she deemed collectables, she found a flower hair clip.
Downstairs, Tommy was sitting on the settee eating rusks and crisps. Mum was in the kitchen, smoking at the open back door. Dad sat at the table looking at the sports page of his newspaper.

"Last day before the Christmas holidays," Piety said brightly.
"Oh crap," Mum said.
"So, no more school?" said Dad. He wasn't paying attention; he was drawing around things on the paper with a biro. Bets for horses, she presumed. "How long are you off for?"
"Two weeks," Piety beamed. "It's nearly Christmas!" she spun around, arms wide.
"Watch out, Pi! You'll knock stuff off the table," Mum snapped. Piety poured herself a bowl of

cereal. "We haven't got much milk left, leave that for your brother. Can you get some on your way to the bookies, Eddie?"
"Why can't you go? You're sat in the house all day."
"I don't do nothing, y'know. I have *him* to look after, and housework to do."

Piety put the milk back into the half-empty fridge. Looked at the piled dishes and dirty plates and pans cluttering the draining board and cooker top. She took her dry cereal into the living room and sat next to her brother. Mum and Dad continued to bicker.

"What you watchin' Tommy-Tum?"
"Digdaw."
Piety watched the big, orange puzzle piece floating on the screen.
"Jigsaw. Do you like it?"
Tommy nodded and sucked a crisp before popping it back into the packet.
"They have jigsaws in our school, y'know." Tommy blinked at her. "Big ones, little ones. You can play with sand too."
"Digdaw."
"Yes, jigsaws. You'd like that wouldn't you?"
He nodded.
"I go to tool?"
"Not yet. When you're a bit older."
"I go tool now."
"No, not now, Tommy-Tum."
"Tool! Now!"
"What's all the shouting about?"
Dad came in.
"Tommy wants to go to school but I told him he wasn't old enough yet."

"Why'd you put that idea in his head? Jesus, Pi."


Each class had its own party and took turns to go to the hall in batches for a disco. Piety wafted her arms and jumped up and down and played run-around like everyone else. The boys ran half the length of the hall and skidded on their knees. The girls couldn't do this because they wore skirts, but Piety tried anyway. The thick, yellow varnish was surprisingly tacky and dragged at her skin. She chafed both knees and tumbled into the front board of the stage. The Hannigan twins jeered and pointed, quickly joined by Richard Burns. Nicole Samson skipped over with Kaylee Jones.

"Why are you wearing your school uniform?" Mike Hannigan asked.

Piety had noticed straight away this morning as she walked through the school gates, that she was the only kid wearing her uniform. Everyone else was in 'party clothes'. Patterns and flowers and checks and stripes. A couple of the boys had waistcoats to match their trousers; like they were tiny grownups. Some of the girls even had blue eyeshadow on.

"She hasn't got any other clothes." Aaron Brockley sauntered over. As usual, Aaron was wearing the latest, trendiest clothes and he swaggered like he was Tom Jones or something.

"I have."
"She wears the same knickers every day," Kaylee said, batting her glittered lashes.
"Eew!"

"I don't."
"Why are you so stupid, Piety Scroggins?" Nicole quipped. "You must have pie for brains."

They all laughed.

"Piety Scroggins' brains are pie, Piety Scroggins is going to cry."

But she wouldn't. Why they had to be so mean all the time, she couldn't fathom. It was worse than those two boys throwing stones. She thought of Saint Peter looking Heavenwards in the big, fat art book, and of The Good Samaritan whom she had learned about in Sunday School. She imagined them all arriving at the Pearly Gates and Saint Peter locking the gates behind him with a massive clang; Piety at his side, 'No room for mean children,' he would say to the six bullies. And they would all cry and Piety would smile because she got into Heaven, and they hadn't. However, Piety did not feel the remotest sense of satisfaction. The thought of them being locked out of Heaven forever concerned her on a far deeper level than she was able to articulate to herself. Where did people go if they couldn't get into Heaven? Wasn't Hell for bad people? Meanness wasn't the same thing, was it? Wasn't everyone supposed to be forgiven? And before she could arrange her thoughts she said,

"Don't worry, you'll still get into Heaven."
That stopped them. Five pairs of eyes stared. Five mouths hung open. It was Nicole who broke the spell.
"You're loopy, Piety Scroggins," she said and skipped off together with Kaylee.

The boys quickly followed, bored of this quarry, and resumed their skidding and play fighting. Piety sat against one wall and watched the rest of the disco. Thankfully, it ended soon after and everyone returned to their classrooms to make cards, hats, and gift labels.

Plenty of glitter and glue, thought Piety as she shaped her cards with pinking shears. Carol tried to show her how to cut the paper neatly, and Fiona and Helen laughed at her attempts. There was a little stack of pre-made shapes; stars, angels, snowflakes and reindeer on the front desk, that you could colour in and glue to the card front. Piety chose an angel. Miss Sparrow sat behind her desk reading a book. Christmas music permeated the atmosphere from a little tape recorder. Some children sang along, heads bobbing side to side. Aaron Brockley pasted glitter stars to his forehead, and everyone laughed, including Piety. Miss Sparrow merely gave him one of those looks teachers reserve for rambunctious children, but she didn't tell him off, because it was Christmas, and no one got told off then. School closed early. Kids galloped through the corridors and playground; their shrieks drowning out the teacher's entreaties to "Walk in the corridor." and "Have a wonderful Christmas."

Piety ran grinning-panting all the way home. Hid her cards beneath her mattress. Clumped downstairs and flopped onto the settee, where her brother sat looking like he hadn't moved since morning.

"Hi, Tommy!"
"Hi, Pi!"
Mum peered around the kitchen doorframe; cigarette held level with her chin. "You're early."
"Last day before Christmas hols," Piety beamed, "we always get out early on the last day of school."
"Have you had anything to eat?"
"We had little butties cut into triangles, and pickles, and fairy cake," she gushed.
"So, you won't need tea."
Piety thought about the seven hours before bedtime at nine o'clock. She would definitely be hungry before then.
"Can we get chips?"
Mum rolled her eyes, "I'm not made of money."
Piety had a picture in her head of Mum made of pound notes and pennies, her eyes blinking in the Queen's head beneath a paper crown. She chuckled.
"What? You think having no money is funny?" Piety shook her head and smiled up at her mum's green face with a pound sign for hair. "I'll smack the smile right off your face."

But later, Piety heard Mum leave the house. When she came back, she'd brought chips. The place reeked of vinegar. It was the best smell ever.

On Christmas Day, Piety received a Cabbage Patch doll and a purple My Little Pony from her parents. A colouring book from her grandparents, which was honestly too young for her, so she gave it to Tommy, and a new dress. And the dress was new!

"A rah-rah dress! Thank you. Thank you!" she gasped, running into her parent's bedroom.

They were still asleep, but this was the one day of the year she was allowed to enter without permission. Mum groaned when she leapt on the bed. Tommy toddled through holding a plastic train.

"Tain!" he chortled.
Dad rolled over. Rubbed the heel of his hand over his eyes and propped himself up on one elbow. "Let's see it then, Pi." Dad was in a good mood this morning.

She ran to her room, whipped off her nightie and pulled on the dress. It was white, with bright pink trim on its five layers. The top was elasticated so that you could pull it down to expose the top of your shoulders. Back in her parent's room, she twisted her hips making the frilly layers swish. She couldn't remember getting anything so pretty, so exotic.

"Best present ever!"
"Like a princess," Dad said.

And before she could stop herself, she hugged him. She could tell he was taken by surprise, but after a brief delay, returned her hug with one arm. She ran around the bed where mum still slumbered, and kissed her cheek.

"Ngh."
"Hey!" Dad called as she made to leave. "You might want these too." He reached under the bed and pulled out another parcel. This was poorly wrapped, with too much tape and no label.
"Who's it from?"
"Father Christmas."

She wondered if Dad was telling the truth. Everyone at school said that Father Christmas wasn't real. They had laughed at her when she talked about him. They said that even the little kids knew he wasn't real. But she decided that they were simply joking and that Father Christmas was real. She pulled off the paper with some difficulty, the packaging was squashed and had too much Sellotape. Inside a shoebox was a pair of white slip-on shoes, with tiny heels. And a pair of opaque white tights with silver sequins.

"Smashing!" she grinned.

Downstairs, beneath a tree that was too large for the room, a hump of gaudy paper was torn free to reveal a bright red tractor. Piety watched as Tommy climbed into the poorly painted seat and made car noises. Dad pushed a button below the steering wheel, and the thing jerked to life.

"Got it off a bloke at work. Dead cheap, a bargain." He grinned proudly.
"Wow!" said Piety.
"Wow," said Tommy.
The tractor lurched forwards and ran over Piety's bare toes.

"Ouch!"
Tommy chortled. Dad grabbed the steering wheel. It reversed into the tree. Something fell off the top and bounced behind the brown armchair.
"Turn the wheel!" Dad bellowed.

Tommy turned and got stuck in the space between the tree and the chair. Dad, still wearing only pyjama bottoms, heaved the tractor and Tommy free. Caught himself across the chest with the raised piece of metal that provided minimal back support. Piety saw the long red mark bloom almost immediately.

"Watch out, Pi."

Tommy howled with laughter as he bumbled back and forth. Laughed hysterically when he crashed into the coffee table, the tree, and Piety. As she stood beside her dad watching Tommy. She craned to look up.

"He likes it, Dad."
Dad nodded and rubbed his chest. "But I'll have to do something about that sharp backrest. Gazzer said the original one had come off. That's just makeshift. It'll do till I get a proper one made."

He headed into the kitchen. He'd never get a proper one made; Piety was sure. He always said he was going to do something but got distracted or was busy with other things. She heard him filling the kettle and putting bread in the toaster. Dad always made breakfast on Christmas morning. The electric tractor was inappropriate, Piety knew this, it needed lots of room. The park would be best, but there was no way Mum would take them. She joined Dad in the kitchen, leaving her brother to watch some kid's Christmas film, still sitting in his tractor. She helped peel potatoes and chop carrots. The turkey sat on the counter looking quite sorry for itself. It had been left out all night to defrost, and now its wings had drooped, and it was an odd silvery purple in parts. Piety poked it with a finger. It felt cold and the pale skin moved and puckered in a way that reminded her of her grandma.

"Go and take your mum that cuppa, would you," said Dad.

Piety walked slowly and stiffly, ensuring she spilt not one drop of tea, and placed it on the bedside locker: adding to the collection of circles there.

"Mum," she whispered. "Cuppa, mum."

No response. Mum snored horribly. On the floor beside the locker was a wine glass. Piety picked it up and sniffed and wrinkled her nose against the sour odour. She looked over to Dad's table, a half-empty pint glass and a smaller glass were squeezed into the small space that already contained an alarm clock, a shadeless lamp, a packet of cigarettes, a lighter, some loose change and a small box. Piety tiptoed around the bed. She picked up the small box. Metal with a hinged lid. She opened it. Inside were a half dozen plastic squares.

"Doo-rex," she read.

She felt instinctively that she had uncovered

something she shouldn't have seen. Something private. Something adult. Her eyes swivelled to Mum still snorking loudly. She placed the box down softly; trying to remember the exact position she had found it. And tiptoed out. She heard the letter box flap open and the soft thump of something landing on the mat.

"Your mum up yet?" Dad yelled from the kitchen.

She descended the stairs and picked up a small package of a plastic bag tied all around with elastic bands. Dad came out into the hall. She instinctively hid the parcel behind her back.

"Oi. Deaf lugs, is Mum up?"
Piety shook her head.
He bounded up the stairs calling, "Ali! Ali! Get your arse out of bed!"

She could hear the soft murmur of her parent's voices upstairs, and at that point, it went quiet. When she opened the package in the kitchen, she found that it was another little troll doll. This one had bright green hair. A card had been folded around it with the words, *Happy Christmas,* written in the same wobbly writing that appeared on the note accompanying the first troll. She went upstairs and stood it on her window ledge next to the other one. They had big black eyes, beetle bright, and the same wide smile. This one had a tiny, knitted jumper. How very odd, Piety thought. Perhaps Father Christmas really did exist.

Christmas dinner went down a treat. Piety liked that phrase; she had heard one of Dad's mates, Fat

Gary, say it when he came to visit; regarding a glass of some dark bitter-smelling liquid. He smacked his lips, smiled and let out an appreciative sigh and said it.

"Ah, that went down a treat," she sighed after scooting her last half potato around the remaining gravy. She patted her stomach, astonished at the firm roundness of it.
"Mmm," agreed Tommy.
Dad seemed pleased that everyone had enjoyed the dinner. "Anyone want pudding?" He stood and collected the dishes. Piety helped.
Mum took a cigarette from the pack at her elbow. "Fetch that bottle of wine from the fridge, will you Pi."

Christmas was the one time that Mum smoked at the table. One before dinner; with a glass of vodka. One after the turkey, with a glass or two of white wine, and another after the pudding.

The room gradually turned hazy grey. The cigarette fumes and smoke from burned oven grease meeting and mingling in the doorway to the kitchen. Dishes, smeared with gravy and remains of green vegetable matter, were piled in the sink and around the kitchen counters. Already there was a small collection of beer and wine bottles by the back door. Mum and Dad lolled on the sofa, pretending to watch a seasonal movie, they kept kissing, and Dad stroked Mum's thigh under her new skirt. Tommy was playing with one of his old toys on the carpet before them. The table was yet to be cleared and put back against the wall. Piety stood between the smoky living room and mountainous washing up. Seeing her brother was happy, she sighed, rolled her sleeves up, and got busy.

There was an unexpected knock at the door.
"Who the fuck is that on Christmas Day?" Dad yawned.
"Pi." Mum tucked her feet under herself and snuggled into Dad.

Piety opened the front door. There stood Mrs Lawler. She wore a navy wool coat with a sort of wrap-around collar, and she had a rain hood on because it was drizzling. She was holding two neatly wrapped parcels.

"Hello, Piety. Merry Christmas." Piety stared. Mrs Lawler swallowed. "I don't mean to intrude, I only wanted—"
"What do you want?" Mum snapped.
Mum was suddenly at Piety's side, yanking her back from the door, barring the way with her body. Piety couldn't take her eyes off the Christmas-wrapped gifts in Mrs Lawler's hands.
"Hello, Mrs Scroggins. I just wanted to give the children a little something…for Christmas…just, you know…"
"We don't need your charity. And we don't need your gifts!"

Mum slammed the door shut. Piety could see Mrs Lawler through the lined glass, standing there. Then she went away, scraping the gate closed. Piety ran up to her room and from the window, watched Mrs Lawler scurrying across the road, head bowed, clutching two soggy parcels to her chest.

Saint Peter's Knickers

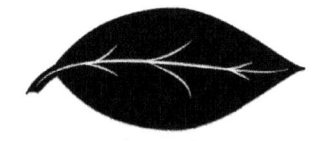

## Chapter Six

"Dad. What do you do?"
Piety swung on the door, holding the knob on either side, leaning backwards at arm's length. Dad was rooting around in the bedroom, opening the drawers and cupboard doors. He knelt to look under the bed.

"Dad."
"What? I'm busy."
"What you looking for?"
"Something. Never you mind." He thumped the wall under the window. "Bollocks!"
Piety repeated the word quietly. Mum and Dad said naughty words all the time, but she was shouted at or cuffed across the head when she did it.
"Dad."
"What do you want, Pi?" he seemed angry.
"In school, we're doing a thing about jobs. And Carol Beverley said her dad is the manager of a shoe shop and her mum works at Littlewoods." She picked at the paint on the edge of the door.
"Good for her."
"Carol said her dad gets all the latest shoe fashions. And her mum — "

"I don't care about Carol friggin Beverley and her shoes!"

Dad lurched past, shoving Piety so she knocked her mouth on the door. She surveyed the disordered room.

"I'm goin' the pub!"
The front door slammed.

"Mum." Piety sat on the arm of the chair swinging one leg. "Mum, what does dad do?"
"What d'you mean?"

Mum flicked through a catalogue, folding down page corners. A length of ash threatened to fall from her cigarette onto the glossy pictures.

"Carol Beverley's dad is the manager of a shoe shop. And her mum works in Littlewoods." She waited but didn't get an answer. "What does Dad do?"
"All sorts." she licked her finger and turned the page.
"Like what?"
"I dunno. Cars."
"He fixes cars?"
"Er, yeah."
Piety thought it funny that Dad fixed cars because they didn't even have a car.
"Carol Beverley says her dad can get shoes for the family at a discount."
"Your dad gets stuff too." Fold. Lick. Turn.
"Does he?"
"'Course he does. What about those shoes he got you for Christmas? And that trike thing for Tommy."

The white shoes didn't fit anymore. And the trike had joined the pile of discards in the backyard.
"Did he get the shoes from Carol Beverley's dad's shop?"
"Fuckin' hell, Pi, you don't half ask a lot of questions. What are you, Little Miss Copper?"

Piety grinned, that was a funny name; like the Mr Men and Little Miss books they had in the infants' classes. Mum stood and carried the book to the phone in the hall. When she bent over to stub her ciggie butt out, Piety caught a glimpse of her knickers where the stiff corduroy skirt had rucked up. She couldn't help the laugh spurt out.

"You've got something stuck to your bum, Mum."
Mum's forehead creased. She swiped at the back of her skirt.
"No. On your knickers." Piety was guffawing now. Her throat made funny donkey noises as she sucked in the air. It looked so funny. "Like a little blue worm!"
"Pi!"
She stopped laughing instantly. Could see Mum was angry. And something else. Her face was all red and sort of tight.
"Don't they teach you anything at school? Don't you know anything?"
"I'm sorry, Mum." She felt her lip wobble.
"Oh, for Christ's sake. Stop crying! Just go away."
"But. I didn't mean anything. Honest, Mum. I just wanted to know what Dad did as a job. And then I saw the blue worm."

Just saying it made her start up again. She could feel the tears on her cheeks and the ache from laughing-crying. Mum gave her shoulders a shake.

"Cut it out!"

The more she shook, the more Piety laughed. It was like being on the jiggly fairground ride at Southport Pleasureland. Mum hit her with the catalogue. Piety ceased instantly. It hurt. The spine of the book had caught her across her left cheek, and she could feel it throbbing already.
"Bloody hell, Pi! It's a tampon. A tampon. You know what one of those is, don't you?" Piety gawped. "It's for when ladies have that special time of the month." Piety continued to stare with her mouth open. "Christ. Periods!"

She shooed Piety away, she wanted to phone her mate Julie to order some stuff. Piety made her way slowly up the stairs. What was a tampon? Why did it hang out of Mum's knickers? And what, she flopped onto her bed, was a period? Crikey, there was so much that she didn't know, when would it ever end?

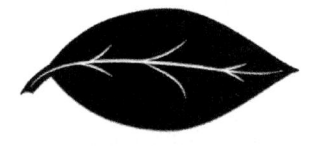

The school librarian collected books that had been left on the tables. Her glasses hung from a chain made of blue crystal bits around her neck. Piety watched the catch of light as Mrs Young bent and straightened. It made her think of stars.

Mrs Young wasn't young. She had tightly permed hair that had some grey at the sides. She didn't smile much but would discuss things Piety had read about. The librarian must be clever, seeing as she had so many books. Piety bet she knew more than Miss Sparrow.

"Mrs Young." Piety rested her chin on the reception counter.
"Yes, Piety?"
"What's a period?"
The librarian looked up sharply. Her eyes narrowed a bit. She peered over the top of her glasses and regarded Piety.
"Have you asked your mother?"
"Not really." Piety fiddled with a stack of brown library cards. "She said it when I said she had a blue worm hanging out her knickers."
Mrs Young looked quickly around the library. She shushed Piety, "Not so loud. I think you should speak with Nurse Halifax. Go on now."

The school nurse sat Piety on a chair next to her desk. She told her all about periods and tampons. She could tell that Nurse Halifax was trying to be clear so that Piety understood what she was explaining, but there was so much about tubes and rooms and blood and complicated words that her brain couldn't hold onto. When she had finished, she sat back and said,

"I hope that helps."
"Do women get their periods on weekends too?" asked Piety as she was about to leave.
"Yes."
"Jesus Christ!"

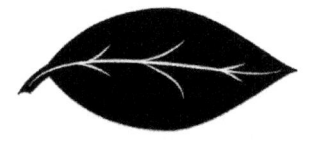

Up in the bedroom she shared with Tommy, Piety pulled a thick book from her school bag. It was square and contained lots of colour prints of paintings.

"Ren-ace-ance," she read, running her finger under the curly white letters. It was probably called the ren-ace-ance because it was ace.

She placed the book in the centre of her bed. Sat cross-legged and opened it to the first image. A trio of fair-haired women in "di-ap-hanus" dresses in the centre with two other figures, who in Piety's opinion, seemed more appropriately clothed. It was by an Italian artist whose name she couldn't pronounce. It seemed like everyone wore floaty clothes in the past, or hardly any clothes at all, it must have been warmer back then, she decided, because you couldn't walk around the Mostyn Estate dressed like that, you'd freeze, the men didn't even wear trousers, they wore coloured tights! Babies were always naked, and women kept showing their boobs!

She thumbed through with care until she discovered the section she was after – El Greco. She looked at a landscape painting that seemed to be something from a dream than reality. The darkening sky and clouds looked about to pour down onto the hills and church and blue-grey stones of a city and swallow them up. She couldn't begin to imagine where in the world this was and how on earth did people even live in such a scary-looking town? Piety thought she couldn't live in a place so haunted looking, so at the mercy of the weather. She stroked her grubby forefinger over adoring shepherds, lonely saints, and dead soldiers being buried in full, golden armour. Portraits of posh people; mostly men, and the Virgin Mary with baby Jesus, and Jesus carrying the cross all by himself. He didn't look too sad about the fact that no one was helping him. Then she found her favourite, *The Tears of Saint Peter*, except in this book it was called something else, *The Repentant Saint Peter*. She made a mental note to look up the meaning of this word the following day.

She looked at the holy one's tear-filled eyes; lots of El Greco's saints had tears in their eyes, but Peter's were the best. They were a sad bunch these saints. Maybe life was harder in the olden days. Maybe they didn't have stuff like Angel Delight, gobstoppers or televisions, or space hoppers, or telephones. Imagine not being able to phone anyone, not that Piety ever did. Mum and Dad hardly ever used the phone, except to call the taxi for the hospital, or Julie for a 'natter', or when Dad was 'making arrangements'. She clasped her hands in imitation of the painted image and tilted her head and turned her eyes Heavenwards. There was something stuck to the ceiling. Near to the corner where dusty cobwebs hung. She climbed onto the headboard using the wall as support to get a better view. How did that get there?

Searching around, she fetched the handle of

Tommy's push-along duck; it had broken off a long time ago, so Tommy wouldn't mind her using it. She poked and scraped at the thing, which finally came away and fell down the side of her bed. Piety retrieved it. It was covered in fluff and crumbs. It was one of those flat plastic monkeys from the game. It had been painted over with white ceiling paint, but the paint had started to flake off. She couldn't remember ever having one of these things. Who'd put it there? She dropped it into her bedside drawer. Closed the book and headed downstairs to see if there was anything for tea.

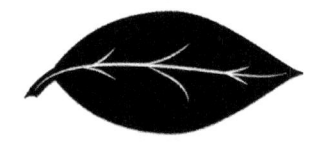

When Tommy started school, they had visitors to the house again. Piety had learned that when adults came to the house, it was usually because something was wrong. Nurse Halifax had never returned, and letters that came bearing the school logo on the white envelope were unceremoniously tossed aside, or binned.

"Mrs, Scroggins. It is Mrs, isn't it?"

The lady who spoke wore a smart navy suit with a bright white shirt beneath. She looked like she had stepped out of an advert for laundry powder. The man wore a dark grey suit with a blue shirt and a darker blue tie. They both carried folders fat with sheets of paper.

"We've come from the LEA to chat about Thomas, is this Thomas?"
Piety held her brother against her legs, hands flat upon his chest.
"Go upstairs, Pi," said Mum. "And take Tommy."
"They can stay if they want, Mrs Scroggins. This isn't going to be a formal meeting, just to introduce ourselves and get a lay of the land, so to speak."

Mum pursed her lips. Piety stayed, in the corner of the room, with Tommy. She didn't fully understand what they talked about. Well, what the blue-suited lady talked about; Mum hardly spoke. The lady used complicated phrases like 'multi-agency assessment', 'language acquisition' and 'sustainable development goals'. She asked to see Tommy's birth certificate, but Mum said she didn't know where it was and blew smoke in the lady's direction. The lady asked when he had last visited the health centre. Mum couldn't remember.

"It says on our records, Mrs Scroggins, that Thomas only visited the clinic on two occasions after his birth. Is that correct?" Mum shrugged.
"It's Tommy," was all she said.

Piety didn't say anything. Nor did the man in the charcoal suit. His gaze wandered around the living room. Piety saw it as though through his eyes, as though for the first time – mushroom brown carpet blotched with a multitude of stains, thin curtains, yellowing nets, empty cigarette packet, full ashtray, a wonky picture of laughing dogs, wallpaper peeling, patched and picked. A forgotten Christmas tree decoration, tossed newspapers, empty beer bottles. His eyes came to rest on the arm of the settee furthest from him, where a mound of chewing gum, pink and white turning grey, had collected. She hoped he wouldn't know it was her who did it. He wrote things down on a writing pad. Piety raised herself on tiptoes, but could not read what it said, and she did not want to get any closer to the people who were asking at what age *Thomas* learnt to talk. *Almost three* answered Piety in her head. *And it's Tommy, just Tommy*. How many words could he speak now? *Not many*. What things interested him? *Colouring books and the TV show, Jigsaw*. How much time did he spend watching the television? *Most of the day*. How many hours a week did they go to the park? *None*. But Mum couldn't answer the questions properly. The two visitors looked at her in silence for a moment before the lady said,

"We have been advised that Thomas has been missing school. He has started school, hasn't he, Mrs Scroggins?"
"Yeah, 'course he has."
"Has he been unwell?"
"No."

A pause. The man and woman looked at Mum. Maybe they were doing that thing that teachers sometimes did. They say something that isn't a question then look at you waiting for a longer answer. Mum didn't say anything else; she just blew smoke in their direction. The man wrote on his pad.

"I see." The woman closed her notebook. "I think that's everything for now." She stood. Her partner followed suit. "Before we go, Mrs Scroggins. Might I

enquire whether there are other family members nearby, or friends who may take on a share of the responsibility?"
"You what?"
"Do you have anyone who can lend you a hand?" The woman's eyes flickered to Piety and back to Mum.
"What for? You tryin' to say I'm a bad mother?" Mum's voice rose in volume.
"Not at all, Mrs —"
"Cos if that's why you're here."
"No, it's about Thomas's, *Tommy's* educational development —"
"Well, you can shove your development. Go on, out!"
They were leaving anyway, so this seemed an unnecessary instruction, Piety decided.

"And you," she turned on Piety after slamming the front door, making the glass shudder in the frame. "Go and read him a book. In your room."

Piety and Tommy scooted up the stairs. She looked around the orange cord carpet. They had no books to read. She had an idea. She sat next to her little brother on his bed and snuggled up close to him. She opened one of her schoolbooks.

"Topics," she began. "Tuesday fifth of October. The Romans."
He sat quietly, so she continued. "In Roman times, children did not go to school." Her brother looked startled. "Imagine that Tommy-Tum, no school. How boring." He nodded. "Some children were taught the skills of their family trade; others were trained to be warriors." He looked up at her. "Do

you know what a warrior is, Tommy? A shake of the head. "It's a soldier. And look, here's a drawing of a soldier from ancient Rome."

She showed him the handout that she had coloured in of a legionnaire. His face was an astonishing shade of pink and the cheeks had gone fluffy where the paper had been coloured over repeatedly, the pen marks rarely contained within the black outline.

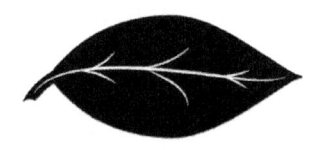

"Can you say, soldier, Tommy?"
"Sow-der."
"No. *Sold*-yer. Sold. Say sold."
"Sowed."
Piety sighed. It was going to take more than the Roman army to get Tommy to speak correctly, she decided.

Following the visit, Mum took Tommy to school every day — at least for a couple of weeks. After that, she made Piety take him.

## Part Two

1978

The world changed when Piety began attending Old Range Comp. For starters, she had to leave the house earlier; the bus stop was at the end of her road and arrived at eight-fifteen, so she didn't have time to sit and watch TV with Tommy anymore. She had to ask Dad to reset her alarm clock, she couldn't remember when it was a quarter-past-eight; she could only tell when the clock hands showed the hour and half-past the hour; all the other numbers were too complicated, so she was always at the bus stop too early. Miss Sparrow had tried ever so hard to get her to learn the time, some of her classmates could even do the twenty-four-hour thing. She and Carol Beverley had sat on a wall once while Carol tried to show her, on her new watch her dad got from Blacklers department store, how to tell the time. But Piety had been distracted by Bugs Bunny's arms twitching around the dial.

It took 106 steps to reach the bus stop. She didn't know how long the bus journey was because she always lost count; there was so much going on. When she arrived home, she had to do homework;

an extraordinary amount of subjects, it made her marvel. Also, there were many, many more kids than in primary school; over three times the amount; she checked this with the school Bursar. They came from all over the place and for the first week she had to try and navigate not only the physical building itself but the grounds and the tangled map of potential new friendships.

It was tremendously exciting, although her friend Carol was put in a different form group, so they only met up at lunchtime now. Occasionally. By October, Carol had made friends with a girl named Susan. Susan was four months older than Carol. She had an older brother and sister and a dog called Pepper. She lived around the corner from the school, so did not have to get the bus. She had chestnut brown hair tied back in a ponytail which swung mesmerizingly back and forth when she walked.
Piety had not made friends with anyone.

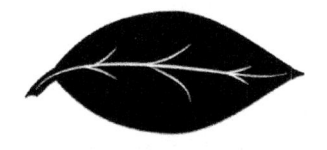

## Chapter Seven

"Aren't the older kids really tall?" Piety spoke around her half-chewed meal.

School dinners were better here. They had a choice! It was amazing. Once a week they had chips; lots of kids moaned that it wasn't more often, but Piety was thrilled to have the opportunity to decide what to eat for the first time in her life. In primary school, and at home, you got what you were given. At Old Range, there were chips, jacket potatoes, mince and mash, pasties, and so many vegetables that she had never seen before. Some of the names made her laugh, like dumplings, cauliflower, and leeks. The funniest was broccoli. It was hard to decide what to have and every day someone would shout down the line to 'hurry up!' Piety liked the dinner ladies, she always said hello and said their names, which were written on rectangular badges on their pinnies. Often, they helped her to select the right things. She always chose too much from the vast array of food set in big aluminium trays and often did not have enough money to pay.

Carol peered shyly around, "Some of them. He is." Her eyes followed three boys who wore the uniform of the Sixth Formers: black pants and a black polo shirt.
"Giants," giggled Piety, spraying crumbs.
"Why did your mum and dad call you Piety?"

This was Susan. Susan didn't much care to spend lunch with Piety. She had told Carol that she thought Piety was 'grubby' and didn't wash her hands before eating. From that moment on, Piety had ensured that she washed her hands after every pre-lunch lesson. She saw Susan looking her over.

Piety shrugged. "Not sure."
"Haven't you ever wondered?" Piety shook her head. "Really?" Susan sounded disbelieving, "You never thought to ask why they gave you such a weird name?"
"That's a bit rude, Susan," Carol said.
"My dad said they wanted a boy, and they were going to call me Pete." She scraped the mashed potato into a little mountain. "Mum saw it written down and her friend Julie said that mine was the girl's version."

She shrugged and continued eating her grey stew of unidentifiable meat with soft potatoes, chunks of carrot and thick gravy. She loved it. When she picked her plate up and licked the remains of the gravy from it, Susan and Carol stared, wide-eyed.

"Mm," she smacked her lips, "Delicious."
Susan pulled a face before shoving back her chair. "I've finished. I'm going outside. Coming Carol?" And off she went without waiting for a reply.

Carol looked at her retreating back, then at Piety. She leant across the table and whispered, "You can't lick your plate like that."
"Why not?"
"It's bad manners. Look, I'm going outside for a bit, see you later."

Piety sat alone in the noisy dining room. It wasn't at all like Beacon Park. It was a much larger canteen with much larger kids. Voices were a cacophony of high squeaks and squeals of new kids like her, and the rumbly tones of big boys and the loud brash blare of teenage girls. Two tables away, she could hear Aaron Brockley regaling a gaggle of lads with crude jokes. She stared at the food Susan had left on her plate, half a sandwich and a small portion of salad leaves. She ate the leaves and put the half sandwich in her cardigan pocket, took the trays back to the wheeled stand and headed for the toilets. She washed her hands. She turned them over in the water.

"They aren't dirty,"

The black under her nails had always been there; it was normal. She squirted more soap out of the dispenser. Sniffed it. It wasn't unpleasant, but it didn't smell of perfume or the soap in the supermarket.

Sometimes when Piety was sent to the shop for a loaf of bread, milk, or loo roll, she picked things up off the shelves wishing she had money to buy them. She particularly liked the smell of one soap. It was brown, but not like mud, more like toffee, and you could see the light through it. Once, she had been chased out of the supermarket when an assistant had found her sniffing soap bars; she had carefully peeled back the ends of about half a dozen packets and sniffed them to see which she preferred. Mum had been cross when she'd returned without t-bags. But Piety had made her mind up that when she had her own house, she was going to buy this semi-transparent soap and have it in a ceramic bowl.

After washing her hands as thoroughly as she could, she entered a toilet cubicle. She had to try and squeeze one out before class because she did not want what happened in Beacon Park to happen here. She leant her elbows on her knees and her chin in her hands. The outer door slammed open, and she heard a gaggle of girls enter. There was the sound of a zip opening and the soft rattle of make-up.

"Have you seen that ragbag in the art class? What a scruff."
Piety wondered who they were talking about. She felt sorry for whoever it was.
"The little one with blonde hair?"
"Blonde? Looks like bacon grease. Can't believe she leaves the house looking like that."
"And her clothes are too big. Why do some parents buy their kids such huge uniforms?"
A laugh, "'cause they'll grow into them," they chorused.
"She won't. She's a bleedin' shrimp. Always will be. Got legs like straws."
They all laughed.
"Have you smelt her?"
"No thanks. I keep my distance. Don't want to catch

nothin'."
"What a tramp."
"Here, try this. My mum got it from Woollies, I nicked it from her handbag this morning." The sound of a hairbrush being dragged through long hair. "C'mon. I got Physics with Connor next. What about you?"
The door slammed open. The chatter faded. Piety sat in silence and chewed her lower lip.

The bus ride home was another challenging situation. On the way to school, there was a constant hum of chatter. She only picked up snippets of conversation — TV last night… lost my homework… number one in the charts… can't stand maths. But going home was a different experience. It was as though someone had shaken a bottle of *R. White's Lemonade* before opening it. Most of the kids piled in like pigeons returning to their lofts, fluttering, and jostling, like the ones that belonged to Billy Ramsey down the road. It was exciting rowdy. It was shoving and pushing and giggling and shouting and swinging bags and little kids crushed between big kids and pulling on people's coats as they climbed the stairs to the top floor. It was thrilling in a slightly scary way. Piety's cheeks ached from grinning by the time she sat down as the tune to the lemonade advert went round and around in her head.

"Get up." She looked up into the face of a girl of about fourteen years. "Move it, nitwit."
The seat next to Piety was vacant. "You can sit here," she smiled.

For Piety, every newcomer was a potential new

friend. If you were all chucked into the same school together, then you had that in common, didn't you? 'Cause everyone wore the same uniform and sat in the same classrooms with the same teachers. And you didn't know if someone else was looking for a new friend too — unless you asked. Some people found it easy to make friends, but she never did. There were those who just kind of fell in with each other or seemed to have been friends forever. This didn't seem to happen to Piety, so she had decided a long time ago that it was best to ask.

The girl bent down so that her face was inches away. "I don't want to sit next to you. I want to sit with my mate. Move your scraggy carcass. Now!"

Rude, Piety thought, but maybe she'd had a difficult day; Mum was sometimes like this after a 'bad day'. The bus hadn't moved off yet, and everyone was staring. Piety stood and shifted out of the way so the bigger girl and her friend could slide in.

"I'm Piety. What's your name?"
The girl screwed her face up as though looking at the most astounding creature on the planet.
"Fuck off." Adding, "Christ you stink, did you piss yourself? I hope you didn't piss on this seat, cos otherwise I'll punch your stupid face in."

Hot spots flared on Piety's cheeks. Little pinpricks nipped her eyes. She swallowed and sucked her lower lip hard. *Pee pee Piety.*

The journey seemed to last forever. Piety would have moved but there was nowhere to move to. The bus was packed. The aisle heaved with boys and girls. All different shapes and sizes. Smaller ones had their faces in the armpits of the taller ones who were able to reach the overhead handrail. At the back, someone was telling jokes; boys bellowed with laughter. Girls chatted with their heads together. She could hear the hubbub from upstairs too. Everyone was with someone else. She watched one girl take a small mirror from her school bag and begin applying mascara. Funny, thought Piety, why would she put make-up on going home? Why did some of them wear make-up to school at all? Another combed her hair; oblivious to the long strands that stuck to the blazer of the boy standing alongside. She had nice hair.

At that moment, Piety noticed the girl at the front. She was small; like Piety, but with long, jet-black hair tied into two shiny plaits. She wore a smart blazer and had a little leather satchel on her back. But what caught Piety's attention was the way she held tight to the vertical bar with both hands and had her back to the rest of the bus. She was pressed against the luggage area staring down intently. And she was alone too.

At home Piety tried to teach Tommy some new words; she had done her homework during the afternoon break. At seven years of age, her brother's pronunciation had shown little improvement; he still struggled with unfamiliar words and couldn't pronounce the letters *R* or *L* correctly. He also took a long time to begin using new words in everyday speech. Piety had once seen a letter from the school recommending Tommy have speech therapy, but Mum and Dad had left it on the growing mound on top of the fridge. There were bills with words in red ink, and another with sections that were meant to be filled in by one or other of her parents.

"Wanna o-ee ice, Pi?"
"Lolly ice. *Lolly.*"

Iced lollies seem to be the only thing her mum kept a good stock of these days, and Tommy ate far too many. She learned from biology lessons that they contained lots of sugar, and sugar was bad for teeth; that's what the adverts said. Toothpaste adverts fascinated Piety; all the animated diagrams of toothbrushes battling invisible food particles. There was one that she remembered from primary school about a kid who secretly ate sweets in bed, and when he went to sleep all these little black devil things came and dug around in his mouth, making his teeth go black and rotten. It left an impression on Piety. She was terrified of the devils coming and digging in *her* mouth, and *always* brushed her teeth before bed. And never ate sweets afterwards. But her brother did.

"Okay, Tommy. I got some new words for you."
Tommy sucked on his blackcurrant ice pop sitting on his rumpled bed across from Piety. "Geography. Say geography."
"Geogwaphy."
She didn't correct him. "Biology."
"Bi-o-ogy."
"Syllabus."
"Sybbabus."
"How to safely light and use a Bunsen Burner."
"For Christ's sake, Pi, let him be." Mum stuck her head round the door. "Think you're the brains of the

family, eh? Leave him alone." She stomped downstairs.

Tommy tossed the lolly stick onto the window ledge. "Bored now, Pi. Gonna watch telly."

Piety sat next to her brother on the settee. She had given up waiting for Mum to cook tea and found two packets of crisps at the back of the cupboard. They watched *Survival* on ITV; an episode called *The Year of the Wildebeest*. She and Tommy laughed to see a young male trot then bounce around on stiff legs, it was a comical creature, with its long face and the funny moaning moo sounds. The herd reminded her of school — a huge pack wandering aimlessly coming together in little clumps — except they weren't wearing uniforms, of course, the big ones bossing the little ones and the boys sometimes having a scrap. Then the screen showed two cheetahs. They moved slowly, sneaking with shoulders rolling high and heads low. They didn't hide or anything, just kind of strolled on into the grassland where giraffes, zebra and wildebeest ate and played. Suddenly, they broke into a run. Piety stopped chewing her crisps. Tommy's hand paused inside his packet. *Run!* She silently urged the calf. *Run! Please get away.* Tommy made a croaking noise as he sucked air. Piety's lip quivered as the narrator's voice said, "*And that is one young wildebeest who will never make the journey that is about to begin.*"
The cheetah had the calf wildebeest around the throat. Then the other one came and bit its legs. It was horrible. She watched as the little wildebeest slowly stopped struggling and then go limp. Why didn't the others help? Why did they all just move

away or stand and watch as one of them was caught? She didn't understand how the wildebeest could do that, just watch as one of their children was killed. Stupid, stupid animals.

And when she cried, Tommy looked up at her and started to cry too. She couldn't see the screen properly, but when the wildebeest started to cross a muddy river, they all piled in like they were getting on the school bus, and the little ones were shoved about, and a crocodile lunged at one. But when it escaped, scrambling up the far, sheer bank and shaking itself before galloping off, Piety gave a cheer, laughing the tears away and nibbled her brother's thigh with a snappy crocodile hand.

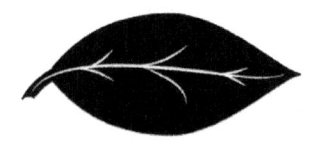

## Chapter Eight

Between lessons, Piety spent most of her free time in the library; occasionally venturing into the playground to stroll the perimeter alone. Sometimes she loitered on the brink of a small group who seemed like they might be friendly, but she was never invited to join them. She watched the boys playing football and tussling, the girls rhythmically bouncing two balls against a wall or playing Double-Dutch with two long ropes. Once, she had asked herself, what if I just join in? and tagged onto the end of a long line of girls to jump the ropes, but she'd got all tangled up and only made them angry. "You need to jump with both legs!" "Oh my God, you're so clumsy." "She can't even jump properly." Were some of the less offensive comments thrown her way. She didn't try again.
The boys were mostly engrossed in their own loud games, as though they owned the playground and took up the largest portion of the space with their frantic games. The girls were relegated to the sides, the older ones tossing their hair and looking round to see who noticed.

Carol Beverley had a new best friend and spent all

her free time with Susan. They walked around the playground shoulder to shoulder whispering and giggling. Susan looked like she thought she was the best thing since sliced bread and laughed exaggeratedly and waved her hand at something she'd said and obviously found terribly amusing or clever. Piety had tried to tag along with the two girls, but after some comments, Susan came right out and said that she wasn't welcome. Carol didn't say anything, she went pink and looked away. That stung. She had thought Carol was her friend, she thought friends stayed friends, how can you just switch to another person like that? Mostly, Piety was alone. It was on one such occasion that she again saw the small dark girl from the bus. She sat by herself, a book open on her lap, and looked, to Piety, like the loneliest person in the world.

"Hello." Piety stood before the girl, "What are you reading?"

The girl raised her head quickly and stared up with the roundest, brownest eyes Piety had ever seen. She looked like someone from a painting. She pictured this girl with an immensely ornate robe and crown and a child in the crook of her arm, also wearing a fanciful crown. She stared. The girl stared back.

"Madonna," sighed Piety.
The girl shook her head warily, and replied, "No, Aamina."
"Ah-*mee*-nah." Piety repeated.
Piety plonked herself on the seat next to the girl called Aamina, to the other's surprise.
"You know, you look just like the Black Madonna!"

Aamina leant away a little. "I don't mean every painting of the Madonna and Child, of course, just this one in particular. And you don't have a fancy hat, I mean a crown. Or a baby. I saw it in the library at my old school. She had angels on her head and, and lots of jewellery. She looked like you. Sad."

The other girl looked at her, down at her book, chewed her lip and frowned at Piety.

"I'm sorry," she said, "I do not understand what you mean."

"The Madonna and Child. Lots of paintings have been done, I like the saints best because they were normal people who did good things by choice. But the Madonna, though she was a good person, because otherwise why would God have chosen her to have his son, isn't like ordinary humans, is she? So, she doesn't count, not like Saint Peter, or Saint Jerome, or Patrick, or — where are you going?"

Aamina stood clutching her book to her chest. "I have to go inside now."

"Shall I come with you?"

"Erm." Her eyebrows squiggled like black caterpillars. She had amazing eyebrows, Piety noted. "I think I will be alone for a while. Thank you." She made a gesture that looked like a small bow.

Piety stood. "I'm Piety!" she called after her. "I'm in class 7B!"

"I'm Piety. I'm in class 7B." A whiny, sneering imitation of her voice.

Aaron Brockley stood a few feet away with another boy. They sputtered laughter.

"What's wrong with you, Scroggins? Peed yourself

lately?"

They wandered off towards the playing field. She heard the boy ask Aaron what her name was, and when he said it, the other boy laughed so hard he doubled over. She had seen Aaron at the start of the new school year, when all the new kids were gathered so they could be assigned to their form tutors. They'd locked eyes across the sports hall on the first day, he held his nose with one hand and made wafting motions with the other. The boys on either side of him had looked over and said something and laughed. They were only in two of the same classes, which was a relief, and Aaron didn't get the bus; his dad gave him a lift home. Piety thought that starting secondary school would mean all the teasing would be left behind. But it hadn't been, and because there were so many more kids here, being alone seemed a bigger problem. Maybe you had to keep asking people if they wanted to be your friend.

She sat for a little while longer staring at nothing. She thought about the girl called Aamina. She hadn't heard a name like that before and decided to head off to the library to find out. After searching, and then asking one of the librarians, she sat with a big book of baby names. The librarian said it had been bought by one of the teachers when they were expecting, then donated it to the school.

"A-a-mina." Piety read. It had taken a surprising amount of time to find the name; it wasn't spelt at all how she expected, and she had to ask for help. "Ar-mee-na. A-mee-na." She read that it meant, *Secure, Trustworthy, Loyal, and a lady of peace*

*and harmony.*
"A lady of peace and harmony." She liked this meaning; it suited the lonely girl. She also read that it was the name of the mother of the Prophet Muhammad.

"Who is the Prophet Muhammad?" Piety asked in Religious Studies lesson.

Someone sniggered at the back. The teacher looked at her as though she had said a swear word. This was another thing about 'big' school that had taken Piety time to get used to, they had a different teacher for every subject! At Beacon Park Primary they had the same teacher all the time; except for assembly, which was taken by the Head Teacher or Deputy Head. Now she had eleven teachers; English, Maths, Physics, Biology, History, Chemistry, Geography, Art, P.E, French, Music, and Home Economics; Piety's Music teacher was also her French teacher. *And* a separate form teacher — who took the register in the morning and after lunch. Sometimes Piety got their names mixed up.

Something light hit her on the back of the head and bounced off. A ball of paper rolled across the floor under the desk next to hers. The teacher offered a stern glance to the back of the room but said nothing.

"Muhammad," began the teacher, "was the founder of Islam."
"Where's Islam?"
"It's not a place, it's a religion. You are in Religious Studies, not Geography."

"So, how did he find it?"
The teacher's shoulders rose in a sigh. "*Founder*, not *finder*. He didn't find it. Founder means he was the person who started it. We did this two weeks ago, Piety. Don't you ever listen?"
"Yes, Miss George. But I can't remember everything."
The teacher went and sat behind her desk. Rubbed a hand across her brow with her eyes closed. "Miss Scroggins. *My name* is Miss Grayson. Miss George is your Chemistry teacher."
Voices, sotto voce, began around the room.
"I apologise, Miss Grayson."
"When you have written something in class, please read it when you get home."
"Yes, Miss George, *Grayson*. Miss. But there's so much to read. In Beacon Park, we didn't have so much to remember, and we only had one teacher, and —"
A burst of laughter exploded behind and to her left.
"Jack. *Please*," said Miss.

The teacher returned her attention to Piety, "Listen to the rest of the lesson. Write down what I tell you. And read it through when you go home. Okay?"
Piety nodded. Miss seemed annoyed. "Good. Then let's continue. I have a clip I want you to watch — Jack Levigne, stop that — and I would like you to take notes in your blue books. In particular — Amy Dunne turn around — the opinions of the neighbours where the conversions are taking place. Hand down, Miss Scroggins, no I do not mean religious conversions, I mean building conversions."

She pushed the video tape into the machine

beneath the TV and the clip began. It was something about how places change when different people, from outside the community move in and the changes they make to buildings because of their religious beliefs — at least that's what Piety inferred from it. She watched in silence and wrote a couple of words down. She found it hard to listen, watch and write at the same time. She was constantly told to pay attention in lessons, but her brain fizzed all over the place. When she tried to give all her attention, she didn't take any notes, and the teachers told her off for not writing anything down. How on earth was she meant to listen and look and write all at the same time? It didn't make any sense. But the more Piety listened, the less she seemed to remember. And because she could not listen and write at the same time, she missed a lot of the work. Other times, she heard the teacher saying her name; quite crossly in fact, and realised that she had been staring at nothing in particular and thinking about nothing at all. Daydreaming, they said. Miss Sparrow had sometimes called her Dolly Daydream, but in a nice way; not like here. Her classwork and homework often went unmarked because the teachers complained her handwriting was 'Shocking, simply shocking.' That was Mrs Waterhouse, who taught history. 'Illegible nonsense.' Miss Burrows called it, before practically flinging her English homework back at her. And 'Something a toddler would scrawl.' Mr Ibsen, geography. Piety couldn't see the problem, she could read her writing quite clearly, and she only exasperated the teachers even more when she giggled. She couldn't help it, sometimes the teachers said things like, it looks like a spider tap-danced across the page, which caused her no end of hilarity.

Mr Whiteside, who taught Biology, became particularly frustrated with her continuous questioning. *How can all those organs fit inside a tiny baby? Why are cauliflowers white and broccoli green? Why is a bean called a bean? What is the inside of the elbow called?* And the one that made him lose his top, as Mum would say, was after looking at pictures of insects and crustaceans when they were doing work about exo-skeletons — *Why don't crabs have eyebrows?* Mr Whiteside had made her stand outside the room for the rest of that lesson. He said she was being cheeky, but she honestly wasn't, she wanted to know, but he didn't believe her. How were you supposed to learn stuff if you didn't ask questions? She tried hard to remember the names of things, but she was not good at the sciences. Miss who taught chemistry, had given Piety a sheet of paper with a load of formulas on it, but to Piety, it looked like someone had tipped letters and numbers across the page. And Physics was another thing altogether. Piety simply could not understand the terminology or what the Periodic Table was all about; it had nothing to do with women's periods. *Why was potassium represented by the letter K? Why was lead called plumbum?* That made her laugh too. Everyone laughed, but she was always the one who laughed loudest and longest and was told to leave the room until she calmed down. Yet strangely, she enjoyed these lessons, genuinely enjoyed them. Even if she couldn't always remember stuff, she was discovering new things every week. The world was an amazing place!

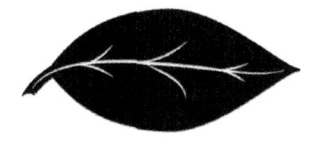

Piety began to seek out Aamina at lunchtime. First, she gobbled her food down before racing into the lower school playground. The quiet girl was always in the same place, always reading. It was strange, she thought, the way no one seemed to bother the girl, nor did she seem bothered about being by herself. She was always very neat, her hair tied in tight thin plaits, and always put things away in her lunchbox in an orderly fashion, she never dropped empty packets on the ground like other kids.

She didn't talk much, but Piety did enough for them both. Talking had always come easy to her, but when she opened her mouth, the wrong stuff came tumbling out, she never seemed to be able to say exactly what she meant, and sometimes this got her into difficulties. Aamina did not eat in the canteen; she brought sandwiches from home and ate outside; she said that she found the canteen to crowded and noisy. Piety asked what she did when it rained, and what was she going to do when winter came, surely, she wasn't going to stay outside. She discovered that Mr Wright, the art teacher, sometimes let Aamina sit in his classroom to eat. Kids weren't meant to be inside during breaks, but Mr Wright said that as she was no trouble, he made an exception. Piety's mum wouldn't make her sandwiches, so when she found jam in the cupboard, she made her own and raced to the art room to have lunch with Aamina.

"Would you like to be my friend?" Piety decided to ask because she wasn't sure still.
"That would be nice, yes,"
"I'm surprised you haven't got loads of mates. You're so pretty."
"I think it's because I am different." The girl's black eyes shone like Mr Ibsen's highly polished shoes.
"Different?"
Aamina held Piety's gaze, a tiny frown crinkled across her forehead and the bit of her nose between her eyes.

Over time, her new friend became a little more talkative. Piety noticed how there was always a long pause before the girl spoke, like she was properly thinking about what to say. She hadn't met anyone before who thought about what they were going to say before they said it, people just talked. They shared books they liked, Piety mostly liked art books with plenty of pictures and fewer words, and Aamina liked novels and even lent Piety a copy of one of her own books. She tried to read it, but there were so many words that seems to run into each other that she kept losing her place, and she had to keep rereading passages, which then meant that she couldn't follow the story. Aamina would read a chapter out loud whilst Piety ate her sandwiches or something the other girl had brought in a neat little yellow box with a clip-down lid. She enjoyed listening to Aamina read, she had a lovely accent, not like anyone she'd met, and not like Nurse Halifax in Beacon Park, she properly pronounced all the words and sometimes it made Piety feel sleepy, so she would put her head on the desk and close her eyes and see all the things Aamina read in her mind.

Aamina was not allowed to stay up past nine o'clock on school nights, so she did not know what *The Sweeney* was; in fact, she hardly watched TV at all. She did not eat ice pops or crisps. She did not go to Sunday School or play in the street. Aamina was the politest person ever. She was also the prettiest girl. Piety would hold her hand next to Aamina's and say that she wished she had the same colour skin, "I look like chalk," she laughed, and Aamina would give her a slightly sad look. Aamina was sweet as caramel, had a gentle voice, listened when she was spoken to, her dark eyes serious and focused, and she never made fun of the way Piety spoke or told her to go away when she got overexcited about something; Aamina would rest her warm hand on her arm and say, in her soothing voice, *not so loud, my friend*. My friend! Piety felt so happy she could float when they were together.

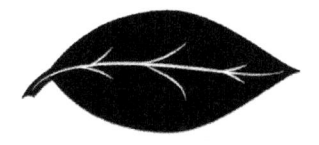

## Chapter Nine

"What's wrong with you?"

The words were flung like an accusation rather than a question. Mum looked like she had eaten sprouts. Piety sidled from the room and slunk up to the bathroom. In the mirror an unfamiliar face stared back - hollow-eyed, blue shadow and lipstick smeared, not like the models in *Honey* or *Woman's Own*. Not like the girls on the bus. She had watched them daily, stroking their fingertips across blue and green palettes and applying the vibrant colours to their eyelids. Spitting on little squares of black and scrubbing tiny brushes in it, applying it onto their lashes. Fluffy brushes, hairspray, hairbands, rosy blusher, shiny lippy, teeny tiny mirrors in little cases that opened with a soft click. All sorts of fascinating treasures. Stuff she didn't have. But Mum did. And so, she ventured into the floral makeup bag left by the kitchen sink.

She had watched Abba on Top of the Pops last night. The blonde one was whom she liked the most. She wore blue eye shadow and had shiny blonde hair — not like Piety's, hers was darker and didn't wave about the same when she tried tossing her head singing *Take a Chance on Me*. She put talcum powder in her hair to make it lighter. She wrapped tinfoil around her school pumps to pretend they were the giant shiny boots Agnetha wore and had on one of Mum's bras stuffed with tissue.

"What's wrong with you? Seriously. You're nearly twelve. You're a total divvy." It was the look on her face and the tone of her voice that hurt — like her bare feet on stones in the backyard that time.

"What's wrong with you?" That's what Aaron Brockley had said the day she met Aamina.

"What's wrong with you?" That's what Caroline Ledsham said when Piety galloped around the playground pretending that she was riding Black Beauty.

What's wrong with me? Why did everyone have to be so mean, was it her fault? She only had one friend; Carol didn't hang around with her anymore. Mum didn't seem pleased with anything she did; Dad didn't seem to notice. Mum was always sticking up for Tommy, never her. Was there something wrong with her? Why did she always make people laugh? In Beacon Park, she had assumed that people found her funny, that they laughed at her antics and questions the same way they laughed at anyone else. But she had come to understand that she was being laughed at. That she was being mocked and teased. Not the teasing between friends she saw, but the mean kind that hurt. She found it hard to do lots of things everyone else could do, like listening and writing at the same time, tying her shoelaces and her school tie, and keeping her books and uniform tidy. Teachers were always saying 'tuck in your blouse', 'straighten your tie', 'fasten your laces', 'stop crumpling your book', 'use a ruler', and 'sharpen your pencil'. She was always told to 'sit down.' Mrs Waterhouse had accused her of having ants in her pants, which Piety had found hilarious and guffawed for ages after. It seemed like no one in big school had any patience. She needed more time to do stuff. Not being like everyone else hurt. And she hurt every day now — except for the times she was with Aamina.

"I am just going to have to try harder." She decided.

Piety started a routine. Every morning, she sharpened all her pencils, whether they needed sharpening or not. She tucked her long blouse into her knickers, so it was doubly held in place. She made sure to wash her hands before and after lunch. She asked Tommy to double-knot her shoelaces. This meant she had to squeeze them off and on again for P.E. She got Dad to knot her tie and never opened it further than she needed to fit over her head. She tried so hard not to shout out in class, or laugh too loud, or run around the playground during windy weather, or almost knock her chair over with enthusiasm when she thrust her hand up to answer a question. Every night, she lay in bed staring at the ceiling, she would talk through her new routine and the things she mustn't do the following day. It was exhausting. On more than one occasion, she was sent to the Deputy Head's office because she fell asleep in class.

"You know, we can't be having this." Mrs Blundell's shiny lipsticked lips puckered. "You need to get to bed earlier. What time do you go to bed?"
Piety shrugged, "Dunno Miss. Sometimes after *The Sweeney*, sometimes before it."
"Well, there you are then. That finishes at ten, far too late for a first-year pupil. And, I might add, very inappropriate viewing for your age. Do your parents know you watch it?"
"Yes, Miss. They watch it too. So does Tommy."
"Your younger brother? How old is he?"
"Eight."
Mrs Blundell wrote something on the pad before her on her neat desk. Piety poked the pot of a small plant near the edge of the table.
"I like your flower, Mrs Blundell. What is it?"
The Deputy Head stopped writing and gave Piety a narrow look. She said some words Piety didn't understand.
"That's Latin for Chinese jade." She put the pen down and looked for some moments at Piety.
"Does your mother work?"
"No Miss."
"What about, Dad?"
"He has different jobs. Whatever his mates can get him."
"Do you have a washing machine at home?"
"Yes, Miss."
"You take Home Economics with Miss Woods, don't you?"
"Yes, Miss."
"Right. I think that will be all for now, Miss Scroggins. Go back to class. And get to bed before *The Sweeney* starts in future. Understand?"
"Yes, Miss Blundell."
Before closing the door behind her, she said, "Oh,

can I stay up to listen to the music at the start, Miss? That's the best bit."

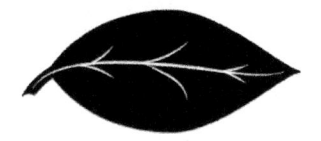

"Aamina!" Piety called a little breathless, "Are you an Arab?" She caught up with the girl with the long black braid near the bus stop.
Aamina looked startled. "No."
"Oh."

Aamina glanced about, wide-eyed looking worried. Piety wondered what she was concerned about. Kids huddled in bunches or were strung along the school railings. Older girls clutched book bundles to their chests, bigger boys with their hands in their trouser pockets, looking like knowledgeable young men on their way home from some office job or other. The senior girls were quite glamorous with hair styled in the latest modes; perms with backcombing, or the Charlie's Angels one; big sideways flicks and sweeps, or the Purdy bob. Younger ones: Piety's cohort, talked the loudest, a couple of boys chased each other around the bus shelter; one received a slap on the head from an older girl.

"Guess what?" she blurted. Aamina did not guess, so she continued. "I've been moved into a different stream for lessons. Not all of them, just the hard ones. I'm in the Remedial Class now, it's a lot of fun, we get to use these tiny building blocks to help with our multiplication tables, and we do loads more drawing than in ordinary Maths lessons, and Miss Woods is showing me how to sew and fix things!"

She heard someone make a rude comment and splutter with laughter. She followed Aamina, who moved away from the main body of students. Her friend whispered,
"Not so loud, people don't understand."

She watched a fifth-form boy take a packet of cigarettes from inside his blazer. A trio gathered around him, and huddled like huge crows, to light their cigarettes. A pretty brunette sauntered up.
"Giz a ciggie, Dale." The tall boy handed one over.
"Ta."
She sauntered back to her mates, who looked amazed and giggled. A familiar voice jeered,
"If it isn't Pee Pee Scroggins."
Piety turned. There was Aaron Brockley.
"Alright, Scroggy, what you up to?"

Piety had never liked being called Scroggy, nor any of the other names the kids at Beacon Park used. She thought, hoped, that she had escaped all that. But no, here it was, all her bad memories, her embarrassments, her childish mistakes, and foibles presented in the form of Aaron Brockley. As if it wasn't bad enough to say stuff in the playground, when it was only him and one friend, here it was in front of loads of people. Most of them she didn't know. Kids from all different years. From the corner of her eye, she noticed a trio of girls sniggering, and heard the word 'Pee.'

"Hello, Aaron," she replied, "I thought you got a lift

off your dad?"
He ignored the question and scowled. "Still pee yourself in class?" he sneered.

His voice was too loud, his grin too delighted. Other kids turned their attention her way, and she groaned inwardly, feeling the heat flare in her cheeks.

"No. Of course not."
"You're in the *Rem's* class now, aren't you?" Huge emphasis on the Rem, he seemed to find this amusing.

She didn't know what to say. He pushed his lower lip out with his tongue and made a kind of groaning sound. She knew this was an insult. She knew this was meant to make her feel stupid, but he did look funny, and she couldn't stop her mouth from curling up. Everyone said that the Remedial class was for the slow kids, the divvy's, the retards, the dunces. Dad had once called her that, dunce, she knew it was meant as a put-down. People were staring, and her cheeks felt puffed — she could feel them getting hotter. Aamina tugged her by her cardigan sleeve until they stood behind two sixth-formers. Thankfully, Aaron Brockley didn't follow. He was distracted by someone shouting "Hey! Broccoli."

"Who is that boy?" Aamina asked when they were ensconced at the end of the queue.
"Aaron went to the same primary school as me."
"He isn't very nice, I feel."
Piety watched her former classmate scuff his shoe in the gutter as he chatted to a boy she didn't know, "He's alright, I suppose."

"Really?" Aamina shook her head.
Piety shrugged, "I don't think he means anything by it. Not really. He's just, y'know, a bit silly."
Aamina gave her a confused look, "You are a very odd person. You are not like other children I have met."
Piety, not sure how to respond, said, "Thanks?"
"Somalia."
"Pardon?"
"I am originally from Somalia. You asked if I was an Arab, I am Somali."

Aamina smiled for the first time since Piety had seen her four weeks ago. It was a wonderful smile, thought Piety. She couldn't help but smile back. Aaron Brockley was forgotten.

"Where is Somalia? Is everyone your colour? Do you have television there? Do you have Angel Delight and Ricicles?"
Aamina did not answer the question, instead, "Would you like to come for dinner?"
"But we've had dinner already."
Aamina appeared to give this some thought, "Would you like to come to my home for food?"
"Yes please!" Piety said.

Piety stared open-mouthed, gawping at Aamina's mum. Mrs Gadiid wore a deep blue headscarf with a brilliant orange flower design. Her skin was fresh and flawless. Her eyes were larger, more almond-shaped versions of Aamina's. She was a stunner; that's what she heard Dad call women on the telly who were beautiful.

"Are you a model?" Piety was in awe.

The beautiful woman had laughed a little, not unkindly, and thanked Piety. But no, she said, she wasn't a model. She was a supermarket assistant. It was the loveliest, most delicious meal Piety had ever eaten. Aamina's mother was an incredibly good cook, unlike *her* mum. Each time something new was placed on the table, Piety said "What's that?" and Mrs Gadiid told her, she didn't fob her off the way Mum did. She didn't know what everything was, but it tasted delicious. Mr Gadiid arrived home as they were sitting down to eat.

"Hello, my girls." He kissed his wife, and he kissed the top of Aamina's head. That was nice, Piety thought, and felt an odd little pang in her chest.

They ate small triangles with minced meat flavoured with spices, a kind of stew with rice, and for afters; or dessert as Aamina called it, a slice of something called halva. This was Piety's favourite thing. When she asked for more, Aamina's mother didn't say 'No! I'm not made of money!' instead she beamed a smile as wide as her daughter's and proffered the plate. Afterwards, Aamina invited Piety to her bedroom.

"Oh, it's beautiful," sighed Piety.

The first thing she noticed was the smell – kind of like the household aisle in the supermarket, but nicer; fresh and perfumed. Every little thing was pink and white, even the carpet was a pale powdery pink, and it covered the whole floor! And so clean. Everything was so perfect, it made her want to happy-cry. She walked around the edge of the room keeping her hands in her cardigan pockets. There was a feeling that just by moving about this pretty palace, the dirt would somehow transfer itself from her to it. She felt suddenly and immensely ugly and grubby — was that how everyone saw her? She looked at a photograph of Aamina and her parents against a foreign background of pinkish sand and trees that looked like their tops had been flattened. All three were smiling from out of the polished wood frame, and Aamina's dad had one hand half raised and was laughing, as though he had just shared a joke with the photographer. She felt self-conscious, everything was colourful and organised and fresh, a room full of lovely things and she, Piety, was a thing out of place. She wanted to touch an ornament here, a colourful bracelet of stones there until her fingers tentatively came to rest on a small painted box.

"You may open it," Aamina said.

She did. A little ballerina popped up on one tiny, pointed foot. Piety made a small gasp. There were rings and necklaces arranged snugly inside.

"It's gorgeous," Piety sighed again.
"It's a music box."
Piety looked at it. "Where does the music come out?"
"Here. I will show you."

Aamina took the box from Piety's hands. She turned a small brass key in the side and the music started, sweet and tinkling. Piety held her breath and listened, it was beautiful, sad, mesmerising, it sounded like hurting and hope, sorrow and peace. It was the love theme from *Romeo and Juliet*, Aamina told her. She watched the little dancer turn round and around, her tiny white skirt stuck out from her body, one arm raised over her head, the other curved before her, like she was waiting for a partner to hold. Piety closed her eyes. When it stopped, she opened her eyes. Aamina sat on the edge of her bed watching her.

"Thank you, Aamina."
"For what?"
"For letting me see your beautiful bedroom and listen to your beautiful music."
"It is only a wind-up toy, Piety. I have music, from my homeland. Would you like to hear some?"
"Oh yes please."

Piety sat cross-legged on the carpet. She daren't sit on the clean white bed with pink, puffy headboard, and the little pile of stuffed toys. Aamina had a small record player; pink as baby clothes, upon which she carefully placed a black disc. What emerged from the speakers was nothing like the music box tune. It sounded like someone was playing the guitar badly, and the singers didn't have soft voices, they shouted strange words. Piety saw Aamina giggling behind her hand.

"What?"
"You do not like it."
Piety knew she should be polite, so decided to say, "Well, not really."
Aamina, laughing, removed the disc, "Me neither." She put something else on.
"I know this!" Piety babbled. "It's on the radio

sometimes."

They sang along to *I Am a Woman in Love*, Aamina holding a pink hairbrush for a microphone, and Piety used the matching comb.

"Do you have your own music?" Aamina asked.
Piety shook her head. "Here, you may borrow this if you like." She held out the record.
"I don't have a record player."
"Oh. Maybe you will get one for your birthday or Christmas?"

Piety shrugged and thought about Christmas in the Scroggins household. She had been washing dishes since she was six years old, and cooking since before she began high school. One year she had tried to prepare the dinner herself because her parents had drunk too much beer and wine to be useful. It was a chicken with two potatoes each, some carrots and watery gravy. Since her dad spent less time at work, there was less money for those 'little extras', as her mum put it. But Piety didn't see Christmas as a little extra. Everyone celebrated Christmas, didn't they?

"Do you celebrate Christmas?" she asked Aamina.
"Sort of." Piety frowned. "It's a bit complicated. My mother is Muslim, and my father is a Christian, so we kind of mix things up a bit."
"Oh."

She imagined Christmas in the Gadiid household was a beautiful affair, filled with laughter, and lovely things. Piety happened to glance towards the window, saw the deep blue square of sky, gasped, shot up and grabbed her school bag.

"I have to go. Mum'll kill me this late." She dashed down the stairs; a gorgeous cream carpet that sucked up all sound. "Thank you, Mrs Gadiid!" she called down the hallway.
"You're most welcome, Piety, do come —"
Piety slammed the door. The glass rattled. She shouted "Sorry!" over her shoulder and ran along the tree-lined street to the main road.

It was only now that she realised that she didn't know where Aamina lived, or where she was in relation to home. When she got the bus to and from school, her friend was already on it or stayed on longer, she didn't live near Mostyn Estate. Buses were going past, but she didn't know which direction she should head. She couldn't remember which way they had walked after getting off the bus. She didn't recognise anything. *Stupid, stupid, why didn't you pay attention!* A flutter of panic began to rise from her tummy and by the time she had found a corner shop it had reached her chest. Eyes prickling, she asked the shopkeeper how to get to Kirk Road, but he didn't know where that was. Luckily, he had an old car atlas which he pulled out from under the counter. He found two Kirk Roads and asked which one was hers. Piety didn't know, but one of them was close to the city centre, so she told him it wasn't that one. Mr Kapani, that was his name, asked her if there was a pub called *The Vale*. This was where Dad went, yes, she knew it! "Wonderful," he said, "then we are not too far away."

Mr Kapani closed his shop and locked the door. He

said he would walk Piety home because he did not have a car and felt unhappy letting her get the bus by herself in the dark. The walk wasn't too long, and she managed to ask him lots of questions. He was extremely patient and didn't once laugh at her or roll his eyes and tut or call her impertinent. Mr Kapani smelt like Mrs Gadiid's cooking and wore a pale blue turban wound on top of his head, it was called a pagri, he told her. Mr Kapani said that he was Sikh, but Piety didn't know what that meant. At one point, he bent to pluck the head from one of the weeds growing from a pavement crack. It looked like the things on the *Shredded Wheat* boxes in Kwik Save. Mr Kapani held it so that his palm edges touched. Then he moved his hands against each other, gently, and the grass head walked up his palm like a caterpillar. Piety laughed and the shopkeeper showed her how to do it. She tucked it into her pocket to show Tommy later.

When they reached the end of Kirk Road, she told Mr Kapani that she would be okay to walk alone from there. In truth, Piety did not want her parents to know that she had got lost and brought a stranger to the house. More than that, she did not want her mum and dad to see a brown man in a turban, her parents were funny about that kind of thing.

"I wish that my teachers were like you. Thanks, Mr Kapani."
"You are most welcome, Piety. And if you get lost again, you know where to find me," he chuckled.

"What time d'you call this?" Mum was cross.
"Where've you been? It's half eight. We've all

eaten, you've missed your tea. God, you're so dozy."

It seemed to Piety, that since she started high school, Mum was always sparring for a fight. She nit-picked about her appearance. She laughed when Piety tried to tie her hair up in a scrunchie with backcombing that one time. She slapped her across the head when the police called to say they had picked up Piety in Kwik Save, for trying to steal a multi-pack of knickers. She let Mum rant without interruption. Sometimes her parents said things like, *you aren't the grown-up, you think you know everything*, that sort of stuff. But grown-ups didn't know everything either, did they? Mr Harris knew maths, but not much about history, and Miss Kearney the P.E. teacher didn't know anything except hockey and tennis and rounders. Grown-ups said stupid things sometimes — just like kids. When her mum said, *you think you know everything*, Piety wanted to retort, "Well neither do you." There was no point in explaining. Anyway, what would she say? 'I went to a girl's house and her mum cooked me the best meal ever, and then we went and listened to music in her beautiful bedroom.' Tommy and Dad barely glanced up from watching the football on TV.

"It's not that late." Dad swigged from a bottle.
"Come on, Tommy lad!" Dad shouted at the television.
"Come on!" Her brother exhorted his namesake.

Tommy had been named after Tommy Smith, Liverpool F.C. defender and Dad's favourite player. It was something they both talked about a lot. She wished she had the name of someone famous. Dad was convinced that her brother was going to be a great footballer one day, just like the *Anfield Iron*. He would sometimes kick a ball around in the street with him and a couple of the other lads. Dad with a can of beer in one hand and a cigarette in the other, exhorting them to 'boot it', and shouting 'foul ref'. Dad encouraged her brother to kick the other lads in the shins and even fight.

They both had furrowed brows, leaning forward with elbows on their knees, straining towards the television. Mum harrumphed. Dad told her to 'keep it down, will ya'. They started arguing. Mum and Dad had been doing a lot of that lately. Sometimes he stayed out all day and night. Once, she had heard her mum crying in the backyard.

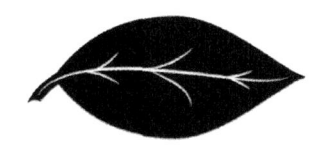

## Chapter Ten

Aamina told Piety that she had come to England three years ago. She said that there had been a war between her country and its neighbour, a country called Ethiopia. Two of her uncles had been killed and another had gone to join the army. Many, many people had been killed. She said that her town was not attacked, but her parents feared that the soldiers would come soon. So, they packed up what they could and came to England. Aamina had cried all the way because she would never see her grandparents again. Because her father was a qualified teacher, he found a job relatively quickly in one of the local primary schools. Her mum had two jobs, she worked in a local supermarket and a care home for the elderly.

"Blimey," sniffled Piety, "That's amazing. I'm sorry your uncles were killed."
"Thank you."
"So, you came here when you were nine?" she counted on her fingers. Aamina nodded. "Did you speak English in Somalia?"
"Sometimes. Sometimes Somali."
"Oo, show me." Aamina said something. Piety

listened to the strange sounds. "What was that?"
"I said, 'Hello, my name is Aamina, how are you?'"
"Can you teach me?"

Aamina tried a few sentences. By the time lunch break was over, Piety had only managed to pronounce the word for 'hello'. She spent the rest of the day greeting people with it.

"Salaam, Miss Grayson," she said as she entered the R.E. classroom. "Salaam, Mr Harris." upon her arrival at Maths. All along the corridors, up and down the school, Piety sang out "Salaam" to anyone passing by. Not a single student returned her greeting; they merely sneered, laughed, or told her to 'fuck off'. Most of the teachers simply told her to take her seat. But upon arriving at her final lesson of the day, the Art teacher; Mr. Wright, replied,
"Alaykum salaam, Piety. Learning Arabic now, are we?"
She halted in the doorway, "No, Mr Wright. Somali. My friend Aamina is teaching me."
"Ah, that would be, Aamina Gadiid, 7A?"
She nodded, "Yes, sir."
"You haven't got any friends, divvy," someone muttered, pushing past, "get out of the way. In or out, make your mind up."

Piety watched Rachael Lamb take her seat at the head of one long table. She preened herself. Tossed her long hair over her shoulder with one hand, tugged at her cardigan until the v accentuated her bosom and chatted to three friends. Rachael was best friends with Caroline Ledsham. They were, taken individually, loud, aggressive, bossy, and rude. As a pair, Piety was not alone in finding them to be the most terrifying pair of students in the school — Caroline had even made one of her teachers cry. Rachael was what Mrs Blundell, the deputy head, called sassy, Piety had heard her say this to her once in the corridor. "Miss Lamb, you have a sassy attitude which is not becoming in a girl your age."

"Well, come on Miss Scroggins," urged the teacher. "Take your seat and we can start. What do you fancy today?"
"Oh, El Greco please, sir."
A groan went up. Aaron Brockley made a farting sound with his mouth.
"Don't ask Scroggy, sir. She always says, *El Greco*." This last was said in a whining tone.
"Mr Brockley, please do not use derogative terms for people in my room. Thank you very much. Okay, gang."

Piety liked Mr Wright. Not because he taught Art, though it was possibly her favourite subject in the whole wide world; she hadn't quite decided yet, but because he commanded respect without being strict. Most of the students liked him. He was easy-going, and liked to 'expand your minds'. He was cool. He had shown her how to wash the palettes and containers correctly. How to wash the brushes carefully so that the bristles didn't get all splayed. He even let her go into his storeroom, so she could arrange the things in neat rows on the green-painted shelves. He had even lent her pencils and crayons so that she could draw at home. He used interesting words, though Piety hardly knew what they meant. Sometimes he played music whilst they worked. This afternoon, she heard a song that the teacher had played before, he was a massive fan of Steve Harley and the Cockney Rebels, and it was *Make Me Smile* she could hear coming from the speakers that Mr Wright had set up in the corners of the room. Mr Wright had told them that Cockney was a name for a certain group of people who lived in London. And a rebel was something he encouraged them to be, "But not on my watch." He added. Sometimes Piety wished that Mr Wright and Miss Sparrow were in the same school, and imagined that her two favourite teachers might fall in love and get married, and maybe even ask her to be a bridesmaid.

"Today, I present for your delectation, la nature morte."
He pulled a thin sheet from the central table to reveal a collection of miscellaneous objects. "Or to you English plebeians – no, it is not an insult Mr Brockley, please do your history research — the still life."

They spent the final hour of the day sketching and painting fancy bottles, a bicycle wheel, a clay jug, some fir cones, and things called gourds. Some of her classmates sang along to the music, Aaron being particularly loud on the *oo la la* bits. After class, the teacher asked Piety if she wouldn't mind washing the pots that hadn't been put away. Piety was pleased to be of assistance.

"Piety."
"Yes, sir?"
"How are you finding Old Range?"
"Er," it was easy to find, thought Piety. The school

bus dropped you right outside the front gates.
"Do you like it here?"
"Oh. Yes sir."
"Seems to have gone quickly doesn't it, these first six months, don't you think?"
"I suppose so."
Mr Wright walked in and out of the stock room as he talked. He disassembled the still life; carefully storing the gourd things in a plastic tub.
"And who else do you know, besides Aamina Gadiid?" He pressed the lid down.
"Well, I know all the people in my class, and Carol Beverley from my old school."
"What about friends, Piety? Have many friends?"
"Er, Aamina and Carol."
He rolled up large pieces of purple sugar paper.
"And what d'you think of Aamina?"
Piety gave this some thought, "She speaks four languages and she's the same age as me! Well, she's twelve, I'll be twelve at the end of June. But that's a lot for someone our age, don't you think, sir?" She turned the washed pots upside-down on the draining board.
"I do. She's very bright. But can I tell you a secret?" Piety nodded, and approached her teacher, wiping her wet hands down her uniform. "She's not as good at drawing as you." He almost whispered it. Piety didn't know how to feel about this. Teachers didn't usually share secrets, as a rule. Certainly, none had ever said she was better at something than another kid. So instead, she blurted,

"She has nice plaits."
Mr Wright appeared to ponder this. "Plaits. Hm, those two braids down her back? That's plaits, is it?"

She nodded. "Would you like plaits like hers?"
"Oh, yes. But my mum says she hasn't time to make fancy shapes with my hair in the morning."
"Hasn't she?"
"No. Because she has Tommy, my little brother, to get ready. He's seven and a half."
"Can't he get himself ready in the morning?"
"Well, I suppose he can, but he sometimes puts things on back-to-front," she laughed, "one day he complained his feet hurt and when we looked, he had his shoes on the wrong feet!" She giggled at the memory.
"Does your mum work, does she have a job?"
"No. She says she's busy enough with Tommy and the housework."
"Well, it is rather a chore, doing housework. But if Tommy's seven, isn't he at school?"
"Sometimes. Sometimes he doesn't go because Dad forgets to walk him and Mum gets up late, and I get the bus early now, not like before when I walked to school, but Tommy doesn't go if Mum is still in bed."
"I expect your mum is tired from looking after the family?"

He paused in the doorway of the stock room, looking at her with a kind of lopsided smile. Piety shrugged, she suspected Mum was tired from all the wine and beer she drank. Aamina's mum and dad had wine when she visited for dinner. They had one glass each, which they sipped slowly between bites and conversation. Piety suspected her mum would have downed the bottle before the halva had arrived. She stared at the floor.

"Are you okay, Piety?"

"I think it's time I went home now, Mr Wright."
"I think so too. Thank you for your help. Oh, and Piety,"
"Yes, sir?"
"You have some paint in your hair." He gestured to the back of his head, "You might want to shower it out."

There wasn't paint in her hair. She asked Mum, but Mum barely looked and told her to stop pestering her. She knelt on the toilet seat and tipped her head this way and that in the mirror. Why would Mr Wright say that? But just in case, Piety stuck her head in the sink under the running cold tap, just in case. In her bedroom, head wrapped in a towel, she shook out her bag preparing to do her homework. Something fell out alongside her books, pencils, pens, and handouts. Piety stared for a moment before picking up the small, white box. The design was familiar; a transparent gold-brown oval. She raised the box to her nose. Took a sniff. Closed her eyes.

"Mm."

Back in the bathroom, she quickly washed her hands with the slippery jewel, before secreting it, back in its wrapper beneath her mattress. As she sat on her bed towelling her hair, sniffing the backs of her hands, a thought suddenly occurred, how had the bar of soap come to be in her bag? She hadn't bought it, nor had she stolen it. Maybe it had fallen in when she was shopping? Maybe she had picked it up and not remembered – her teachers did tell her she forgot things. The only conclusion was that someone had deliberately put it in her bag. But who? She knew that she didn't smell like other kids. She knew from bitter experience that she must smell bad; although she didn't notice this herself, so wondered what she smelt like to other people; 'Cabbage Patch' was a name she had acquired since the new toy dolls had hit the market. Carol Beverley always smelt like Vosene shampoo and Parma Violets. And Aamina's house smelt like an advert for laundry powder and foreign spices. By the time her hair had dried, she had concluded that someone was telling her to get a wash. Someone was being mean. It made her sad and embarrassed, she couldn't help it, she washed her hands every day. Eventually, she fell asleep wrapped in a damp towel and soap scent.

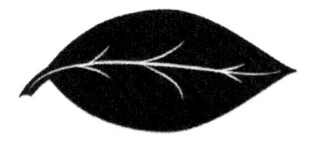

It was bound to happen at some point. When Piety believed that she had thrown off the bullying shackles of primary school, and the bullying died down at Old Range, it returned as a heavy thunk to the back of her head.

She'd never been dexterous; her handwriting attested to this – it drove her teachers insane – "Piety, there are lines on the page for a reason," complained Miss Grayson. They weren't the only lines she had difficulty staying inside. When outdoor games season began Piety was delighted. Running across the field, she was followed by hoots of derision and the shrill peep of the teacher's whistle.

"Get back on the track! Miss Scroggins! Get back!"

She swerved like a nectar-drunk honeybee, crossed three white-painted lines; almost colliding with another student and skip-jumped along the inside track. Tennis. That was the worst. She simply couldn't hit the ball.

She swung her racket with gusto. Whacked air. Laughed despite it all. And then, thunk! She thought her eyes would pop out and fall on the floor at her feet.

"You're bloody hopeless."

Caroline Ledsham shouted from the neighbouring court. She swung her racket overhead, tossing a ball high with her other hand. Piety watched in admiration — the stretch of the girl's body, the way she tossed the ball up and reached, the accuracy with which the racket contacted the fuzzy yellow orb. Thunk!

"Oof."

Piety folded forwards as the ball struck her dead centre of her breastbone. It was astonishingly painful.
Caroline struck a pose. Hand on a cocked hip, the other held the racket over her shoulder. Rachael Lamb stood at her side, a smug grin on her face. Piety rubbed her chest and the back of her head.
"What d'you do that for?" she called.
"Why don't you go back to the library, Scroggins."

Caroline walked closer as she talked. "You can't play tennis, you can't run, you can't catch a ball." Now she was a simple stretch away. "You ruin P.E. every time. No one wants you on their team," She bent forwards from the waist, until her face was a few inches from Piety's, "You're a spaz, a waste of space."

Rachael sniggered and sneered. Piety swallowed. Caroline was easily a head taller than her, all long hair, legs, and prematurely developed curves. What had she done to rile Caroline so much? Why did it matter whether she could hit a ball or not? Piety was confused.

"I don't understand. What've I done to annoy you, Caroline?"
The taller girl snorted. Like a horse thought Piety. It made her smile.
"You laughin' at me?" Caroline snarled through clenched teeth. Piety shook her head. "I'll smack the smile right off your face. You smelly little wretch."

And Piety heard her mum's voice in her head. *I'll smack the smile right off your face*. Mums shouldn't say stuff like that to their kids, should they?

"You shouldn't say things like that, especially if you want to be a mum. It isn't nice."
Caroline and Rachael gawped. And Caroline jabbed her finger in Piety's sternum.

"Rem!"

They sauntered off, sniggering and flinging

disgusted glances over their shoulders. Piety rubbed at the sore spot on her chest, Caroline had super strong fingers, that must be why she's so good at sport, Piety mused. When she turned back to her own game, she saw that the girl she had been partnered with had gone.

In the changing rooms, everyone was obliged to shower. Some of the girls; especially the ones who already wore bras, simply sprayed body mist and dressed. It was *the* most embarrassing situation in high school. You stood with fifteen other girls, naked and shivering beneath pathetic squirts of water from fixed shower heads. Some ran through so they barely got wet. Miss Kearney, who took P.E., would sometimes check the girls had showered. Once, she forced Piety to remain until she had washed. Stood there, arms crossed, and watched! Piety was mortified. She had no soap or shampoo, so the teacher had to loan her some. Plus, everyone could see how flat your chest was.

Piety emerged from the tepid shower room, dishevelled, soaked and shivering. Most everyone else had gone. Piety did not have a towel. She recalled the day she went to the swimming baths when she was at Beacon Park — why did she always forget her towel? She would have to get dressed wet. Two girls chatted in the far corner as they redid their ties. She tiptoed to her bag and clothes. Her shirt was gone. So were her socks and shoes.

Piety padded along the corridor towards her next lesson, pulling her cardigan and blazer tight around her. Students laughed, pointed, and called her

'Rem'.

"Miss Scroggins. Why don't you have shoes and socks on?" Mr Whiteside shooed her out of the classroom. "Where are your shoes?"
"Sir, someone must have taken them." she swallowed down the lump that swelled in her throat.
"Why would someone take your shoes?" His voice had that horrible flinty quality that made it sound like it was her fault.
She shrugged, "They were gone when I came out of the showers."
"And your shirt too?" She nodded. He sighed, "You can't wander around the school half-dressed. Go and see Matron or the Bursar. They'll have some pumps or something, I'm sure."

As the door closed slowly behind him, she heard the shrieks of laughter. It stung like the tennis ball hitting her head. It hurt as much as the bruise on her breastbone. By the time she reached Matron's office, Piety was openly weeping. Matron sighed, rolled her eyes, and tutted. She rummaged in a box before presenting Piety with a pair of too-large black plimsolls and an oversized shirt.
"Make sure it gets a wash before you return it this time. Well, put it on. Off you go."

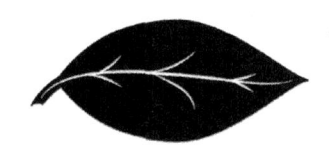

## Chapter Eleven

Piety's twelfth birthday passed with little celebration. Her parents gave her a card; late, and a cheap make-up set. They were drifting farther and farther away from, not only each other but her. Or was it she who was drifting apart from them? When Tommy turned eight, Mum reluctantly took them to the community centre. It had something to do with the local church, but anyone could use it. They had music, a couple of snooker tables, darts, and a bouncy castle in the back garden area. Three of Tommy's friends were invited and seemed to enjoy themselves. But Mum wouldn't pay for more juice and crisps after they'd had sausage and chips and a bag of crisps each. Her brother sulked in the bouncy castle and refused to engage in anything resembling play. Piety felt bad for him. He had wanted an Action Man, and instead got a cheap knock-off version; Dad had a friend from the pub who regularly sold goods that were cheap imitations; like the hideous perfume Mum wore. Sitting on the opposite side of the table, surrounded by the aroma of chips and cigarettes, she could smell the cloying sweet odour.

Her dad was off somewhere doing something she had no clue about. Dad was always nipping out at odd hours. Sometimes he didn't leave the house for days. She knew that he 'signed on,' but wasn't sure what that meant. She knew that the dole was for people out of work, but Dad was always saying he had a job on, so why did he need the dole? She tried asking once and Mum got angry, grabbed her, and told her to *never* tell anyone her dad was doing odd jobs. That had left a little string of round bruises on the underneath of her arm. She watched other mums wiping ice cream off chins, ruffling hair, and dads laughing, waving, and encouraging their kids to "bounce higher", and "do a somersault". One dad was teaching his son how to play snooker. She wondered why her mum and dad didn't behave like that. Tommy scowled. Mum puffed on her cigarette.

She didn't have a word for it, nor a coherent idea about why her family were the way they were, but she knew for the first time, something was different. In Beacon Park, no one knew anything about each other outside of school. In primary school, you were just you. A rag-tag, muddle of boys and girls with no idea of anything beyond the school gate or your own road, tossed together like a can of Pick-up-Monkeys. In high school, kids were from different places and talked about a home life that sounded foreign to Piety. In big school, some kids spoke differently and looked like they knew everything and everyone. No one galloped around the playground anymore, and people kept saying things like 'You're too old for that,' like there was some unspecified age when you were meant to stop playing. Some people ate at a dining table every night; not just Christmastime; the whole family, together — it was a revelation. Her family ate in shifts, like at school. Dad and Tommy sat at the tiny kitchen table, or sometimes Tommy ate sitting on the living room window ledge, plate balanced on his knees. Sometimes, they all sat in the living room watching the telly and eating from plates on their laps. No one talked, not like Aamina's family.

"Go and get us a beer, Pi."
Piety glanced toward the bar. There was a queue.
"It's busy."
"Well go and wait! Christ!"

The money slapped into her palm. Piety joined the queue with her head down. She watched her mum suck her cigarette, and flick ash onto the floor instead of into the ashtray provided, wriggling her buttocks down further on the seat so that she looked like a surly teenager in class. *She's like a kid,* Piety thought. Worse. She's worse than some of the girls at school, 'cos she's a mum and mums should be kind to their kids, shouldn't they? Aamina's mum wouldn't forget a proper birthday party, I bet. Aamina's mum wouldn't swear at you, or slob around chain smoking. She instantly felt guilty for thinking that way. She returned with a glass of Carlsberg.

"What's wrong with *your* face?" Mum spoke around exhaled smoke. Croaky.
"Nothin'."
"You could make more of an effort. Could have worn some make-up."
"I'm twelve, Mum. I'm too young for make-up."
"Don't be fuckin' stupid. I was wearin' make-up at your age. Boys love it."

"I'm not interested in boys." Piety sank further into her coat.
"And they won't be interested in you with a gob like that." Suck. Blow.
"And why aren't you wearing the shorts I bought you?"
"The yellow ones? They're too short and tight."
"Don't be daft. I suppose you want one of those bleedin' flowery maxis down to your ankles. Cover you up." Suck. Blow.

Piety thought maxi dresses were pretty. Mum was wearing huge flares today, and a tiny tank top that she let ride up to show her tummy. Mum wanted a fur coat like the girlfriend of Mick Jagger, but Dad said they were hard to come by. She could see Mum inspecting what the other mums wore with a curl of her top lip. Other mums wore sensible clothes, calf-length skirts with nice blouses and cardigans, or pantsuits. Mum did look very cool; she was definitely the most fashionable person there. She made comments about how dull this one was, or ugly that one was. She sniggered at what she called *old lady clothes* and *ancient haircuts*.

"No wonder their kids are fuckin' ugly." She commented.

By the end of a dreary fun-free day, Piety had made up her mind. Mum was a horrible, horrible cow.

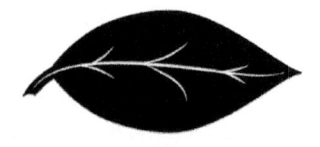

She continued to enjoy lessons; though she understood less than her peers and for some unknown reason seemed to irritate classmates and teachers alike. Piety often stayed behind to catch up with work, it was preferable to doing it at home. Sometimes she worked alongside Aamina.

"What you working on?"
"Maths," replied Aamina. "And you?"
"Same."

Piety was in the Remedial class for maths, but it was still hard, despite the teacher trying to make things fun. She couldn't seem to hold all those numbers and wiggly shapes in her mind. Digits danced across the page. She had to pin them down before she could start doing whatever she was meant to do. Miss said she needed to concentrate more, but the more she stared at the page, the more the numbers shifted. Formulas made her head spin. Fractions may as well have been a foreign language. She made piled of coloured blocks on her desk to count when she did her times tables, and Miss would look impatient, but she didn't have enough fingers and she couldn't remember anything by the time she got home.

"I just don't get it," she sighed.
Aamina smiled her lovely smile, "I find it interesting. You know, in maths, there are rules to follow, it is

logical, not like English. Who is to say that one person's story is better than another's? Beyond correct grammar of course."
Piety gave this some thought. She looked at the scrawl of inky numbers that she had written. It didn't look anything like Aamina's beautiful script.
"Shall I help you?" Aamina said.

But when Aamina had finished explaining and showing her examples, the information seemed to vanish from her head. It poured in one ear and out the other, as Mr Harris often said. Mr Connor, who taught physics, said that he could see the 'blinds come down' when he tried to clarify stuff. It was like her ears and brain kind of tuned out all by themselves. Teachers quickly gave up trying to help, even in the remedial class, because they said they had to move on to the next topic on the syllabus. So she would fill the margins of her books with swirls and stars and horses, then was reprimanded when she hadn't done any work.

Piety often turned up for school in the same unwashed clothes. She had tried using the washing machine herself, but something had gone wrong and all Dad's white undies and Mum's white knickers came out not white and sort of wiggly and small. Mum had a fit. Sometimes, the school dipped into its lost property. And for one glorious week, she wore trousers. She didn't mind a bit. It covered her further.

"You look like a boy." Aaron Brockley laughed.
"Lesbian." Caroline and Rachel sneered.

But the comments became fewer. And she was

able to sit at the back of a classroom and gaze out of the window in peace. At the bus-stop one day, Caroline Ledsham and Rachael Lamb approached.

"You aren't friends with this loony, are you?" Caroline challenged Aamina. Both towered over Piety and Aamina.
Piety saw Aamina's eyes go wide. "Y-yes."
"You know she's got lice?" sneered Caroline, looking Piety up and down as though she had been vomited up by some animal.
"And fleas!" added Rachael.
"I haven't," Piety cried.
"Everyone knows. Fleas and lice. She never gets a shower, so she's got a nest of bugs in her hair."
Aamina looked at Piety's head.
"I haven't." Piety repeated, but Aamina took a step back, staring.
"And she pisses in her pants." Caroline sniffed.
"Ew!" they chimed in unison.
"True," Caroline said. "All her class have said so. And she did it in art class, and the playground. And she gave someone scabies in her old school, they were in hospital for weeks, everyone knows."
"That's not true! It isn't."
"But your skin's probably extra tough, takes more biting to get through all that brown," Caroline said to Aamina. "My dad said that you have thicker skin than white people. He said you should all be sent back where you came from."
"Povvo's and darkies stick together. You shouldn't be allowed near normal people." Rachael sneered.
"Fleabag." Caroline laughed. "And I heard she eats her own snot." More laughter.
"Why do you even bother coming to school, Billy No Mates?"

The bus pulled up. Aamina hurriedly joined the rowdy queue.
"Aamina?" Piety caught hold of her friend's arm. "Aamina. Aren't we doing our homework together?"
"I have to... do something... I have some difficult maths." She was at the steps and Piety released her hold; Aamina was crying. So stunned by the tears, Piety forgot to get on the bus.

The persecutors strolled away, grinning and laughing loudly. Piety watched the crowd shove itself through the doors, into seats, and up the stairs. She watched Aamina stand by the luggage compartment and take hold of the silver pole. The doors hissed air and closed. Piety held her friend's apologetic gaze until the bus moved off coughing dark grey fumes all about her. Her chin trembled. When she turned to watch Caroline and Rachael, her stomach felt wobbly, she felt sick, and her heart thumped rapidly. They shoved a kid as they passed, and she heard Caroline say "Turd." It was Aaron Brockley. He was staring at her but didn't shout anything or laugh or do any of those things he usually did to her. He simply turned away as the next bus arrived.

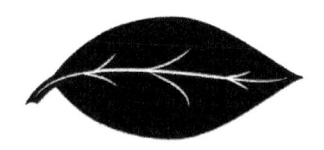

## Chapter Twelve

Piety learned how to become invisible. She spoke less and less in lessons, stopped asking 'stupid' questions, and complained of menstrual cramps when they had P.E.; although her menses had not started, so she could avoid group activities.
Her hair hung in a lank shiny veil about her face, creating a rash of raw spots across her forehead and cheeks. Mum often forgot to do the laundry, or 'couldn't be arsed' Dad said, and Piety wasn't allowed to use the washing machine. She hand-washed her knickers in the bathroom sink, leaving them to dry on the bedroom window ledge — a row of too-small, grey triangles, collecting holes and trailing perished elastic. Her two school shirts became stiffened and yellowed beneath the armpits, her single skirt spotted with spilt food and shiny streaks where she wiped her hands. The treasured bar of soap remained beneath her mattress, taken out once a week at first, then less as she saw its dwindling form and feared it disappearing. Mum seemed more distant than ever, and she barely spoke to Dad anymore. They'd had an argument one night when they came home late, about a woman in the pub. Piety hadn't understood what it was about, just someone called Helen.

She wasn't at all surprised when she arrived home to find no food in the house. Or that her mother and Tommy had already eaten; sausage and chips from the chippy. And Dad was absent, probably at the pub. She found a half-empty box of cereal in the cupboard. Ate it dry from the box, standing in the kitchen. She dropped her school bag onto her bed and left the house.

There were four weeks left until the end of the school year. Four weeks until a summer of idleness, and loneliness. She had not spent time with Aamina since the horrible day at the bus stop when Caroline and Rachael had called them names. She didn't understand why Aamina was avoiding her — did Aamina believe those things they had said about her? She walked quickly to the end of the road. Past the row of local shops – newsagent, Kwik Save, bank, chemist, florist, and bakery. She scuttled past the discount supermarket. Only two weeks ago a member of staff had caught her with a packet of *No-Frills* lemon bonbons in one pocket, and a pair of twenty denier American Tan tights in the other. The man had let her off but said he didn't want to see her in there again, or he'd call the police.

Beneath the railway bridge, along the A-road, a gaggle of teenagers barely gave her a second glance as she passed. A miasma of lighter fuel and Cow Gum surrounded them, and when one held out a paper bag saying, "Wanna sniff?" Piety shook her head and hurried on. She didn't know where she was going. All she wanted was to walk and forget. Forget about Caroline and Rachael and

Aaron. Forget about her mum and dad. Forget about her filthy clothes and the house she was now, after visiting Aamina's, embarrassed by — was that how everyone else lived? She wanted to forget that look on her friend's face as the bus pulled away.

Between the Mostyn Estate and Meadows Hall, beside the A-road, sat a large clump of land dotted with thistles, spindly dirt-covered shrubs and electricity pylons, surrounded by wooden split rail fencing. There always seemed to be birds; crows or magpies, strung from one of the fences. Kids said it was a local madman who had a deep hatred for all things that could fly, so he caught and strangled the birds with his own hands, before tying them with parcel string to the top rail as a warning to other birds. Piety used to stare at the pathetic creatures every day on her bus ride home. There were always plenty of crows in the area, so maybe they didn't understand, or care about the madman's hatred and warning. She'd never seen anyone on this land, if people walked the A-road, they used the narrow path on the opposite side.

She found herself walking her school bus route, but instead of using the pavement, she walked along the fringe of land between the road and fencing. The ground was knobbly with molehills and patches of nettles. At the dead bird fence, she halted. Today there were the carcasses of one magpie, one crow, and as though for a change of some sort, a rat; the rat was dry and shrunken. All three creatures had wide sockets where the eyes used to be, and little bits of bone the colour of rice pudding showed through fur and feather. Piety found a stick and gave the crow a prod. It swung, leaf-light and stiff. This, she reflected, was her. Shrunken, withered and unattractive. She wanted to remove the three bodies, but had nothing to cut them down with, nor did she want to touch the fuzzy brown twine about their withered necks.

A little further on, she climbed over the fence and wandered across the wasteland. Overhead, crows circled and chattered. Bits of white thistledown stuck to her skirt and school blazer, and the thistles scratched at her legs. Apart from a miserable brown pond, there was nothing of interest here. A bit like her life came the thought.

She crossed the main road and headed towards the narrow olive-green ribbon of the river Alt, which she easily leapt, to continue through what turned out to be a farmer's field. Row upon extending row of dark green leaves sprouted from lines of banked-up earth. She didn't have a clue what was growing here, but she suddenly remembered the little plant she had moved from the wall to a *Smash* potato can that her art teacher had let her have – it had grown leggy and tall in the intervening years and for a couple of weeks a year, in spring, it sprouted a small spray of lilac flowers. Piety stared at the lush green ranks before her. She felt guilty and sad that she had neglected her own bloom. Mum had wanted to chuck it out, but Piety had protested so vehemently, that her startled mother had backed down for once.

"Hello little plants," she called across the field.

She crouched and dug her fingers into the dry outer

crust of soil, the tips of her fingers cooling as they touched the dampness beneath. She was surprised by the pleasant smell. She couldn't describe it, but it smelt fresh, clean. When she stood up again and put her hands in her blazer pocket, she found ten pence there. She had found it on the windowsill in the living room. There were always bits and pieces lying about the windows; not like Aamina's house, which was clean, fresh smelling and simply but beautifully decorated. Sweet wrappers, small parts of broken toys, and sometimes mechanical parts that she didn't know what they were, infested the windowsills and shelves of the Scroggin's house. And spare change. She missed her friend dreadfully. She couldn't understand why they had drifted apart — maybe she really was the stupid person everyone said she was. Maybe she was so bad that even a kind, polite girl like Aamina didn't want to be her friend. Piety sniffed and wiped her eyes on her sleeve. Everything had gone wrong. Caroline Ledsham had ruined everything. On a whim, she ran to the nearest bus stop.

There were only a few people on the downstairs deck of the bus. So, when the large woman with a tan handbag over one arm, and a plastic shopping bag over the other got on, Piety couldn't fail to see her. The woman sat in the front seat. Piety stared at the back of her head where sunlight glinted off polished black curls. She did not recognise the woman at all but was suddenly and confusingly overwhelmed with emotion. Her heart felt as though pierced by an arrow; like Saint Sebastian, a bitter-sweet pain. Her eyes welled up, and Piety believed she was witnessing an angel.

*Perhaps*, she thought, I *am having a religious experience*. Piety hadn't attended Sunday School since leaving Beacon Park. It turned out that Mum had sent her and Tommy so they would get out of the house on Sunday mornings, not because she had any great love of the church. Why they had to get out was anyone's guess, but they didn't have to go anymore. Funny, she mused, it was around the same time that Dad stayed out on his own on Saturday nights. Had the angel been sent to make her go back?

She frowned out of the side window, her eyes not seeing much of anything. She watched her breath bloom and dissolve and bloom again on the glass, her heart pounded. She looked at the woman with sunlight all around her. A small cry almost escaped her mouth, till she remembered where she was. When she let her head droop, two fat splots appeared on her school skirt. Piety hurriedly wiped her face. She wondered why the angel was on a bus. Where were her wings? Maybe, like that old black and white film they showed on the TV at Christmastime, she had to earn them? She wondered why the angel needed shopping bags but supposed that even angels who were on earth had to eat. Each time she looked at the large lady, overwhelming compassion and comfort surfaced, and Piety had to look away quickly and chew her ragged thumbnail to prevent herself from blubbing. It was peculiar and inexplicable, what she was experiencing, like when you dream that someone is knocking on the door and then as you wake up, you can't hear the dream anymore and someone is really knocking on a real door. The angel seemed to exude calm and warmth.

When she stood to disembark, Piety followed. It wasn't that she made the decision, there was no thought to her action, it was as if an invisible line tethered them together, gently urging her off the bus. Her legs just stood up by themselves and her feet moved forward. The bus hissed and squeaked behind her before pulling away. The angel was standing there on the pavement. Waiting, it seemed, for her.

"Piety Scroggins?" said the angel with a divine smile.

A key turned in a lock somewhere in her head and something popped open. A tiny, hidden box that connected to her heart. It felt like something had pushed on her tummy and squeezed everything into her chest, the air hissed out her nostrils: baked biscuits warm from the oven, a mustard jar filled with tiny purple flowers, bubble baths, a patchwork blanket — and a pink cake with a single candle. A surge of emotion overwhelmed her. Piety's face crumpled.

"Aunty Nell?" her voice squeaked as though she hadn't spoken for ages.

"Oh, dear. I made you cry. I'm so sorry, chicken." The woman fetched a paper handkerchief from her handbag, "Here."

Piety took the proffered tissue, blew her nose, and wiped her eyes. The woman enclosed her in the biggest embrace and held her for a long moment. How could she have forgotten? Aunty Nell had cared for her when she was small. 'Taken into care' tumbled over in her mind. One day she had been at home with Mum, the next she had been at Aunty Nell's place. *She* was the origin of those misty memories; of all the kindness she'd experienced before starting school. Nell had, Piety realised, planted a tiny seed all those years ago, this is love, this is what it feels like, *this* is how we care for children.

They sat on the wooden bus stop bench and talked. At least, Piety talked, 'Aunty' Nell listened as she held Piety's small chill hand in her own. Piety stared at the floor as she spoke of her family, school, the bullying, her loneliness, the loss of her friend, the picture of Saint Peter, and her little brother. All erupting from a dam of pent-up sorrow she barely realised she carried.

"He's not the same anymore, Aunty Nell," she sniffed, "he used to be my sweet little Tommy-Tum, and now he's like…a stranger."
"People change. And everyone feels sad sometimes, petal," Aunty Nell said, "And that's okay, it's normal." Her voice was rich as dark chocolate and made Piety feel safe somehow.
"I thought you were an angel."
The woman raised her eyebrows, "Now why would you think that?"
Piety shrugged, "You made me feel… protected. Like when I look at the painting of Saint Peter, kind of sad but warm." Aunty Nell remained silent. "Saint Peter is my favourite, he looks sad and peaceful at the same time," she sniffed, "and when I met Aamina, she looked like the Madonna from some of the paintings. She's so pretty, and kind and..." Piety

broke into sobbing again, "I miss her, Aunty Nell. She's my only friend. Nobody else likes me. They all think I'm stupid and make fun of me, and laugh at my clothes because we can't afford what they have, and the teachers don't like me, apart from mister Wright, who teaches art, and I can't do anything right, and Rachel Lamb and Caroline Ledsham pick on me for no reason, and I don't know what I did to make them hate me so much."

Aunty Nell said nothing. She put her arm around Piety's shoulders, pulled her close and simply held her tight. After a while, Piety felt better.

"Can I come and visit you?" she asked.

The woman's round, brown face took on a sad look. "I don't know if that would be wise, petal. I looked after you when you were a little tot, and that was through Social Services. I do not think that it would be allowed." Piety blinked, "However," Piety brightened, "I will see if I can find out what the correct procedure is. Okay?" She patted the back of Piety's hand. "You know, you have grown into a pretty young lady," Piety made a snorting sound. "I mean it. Have you looked into a mirror recently?" Piety shook her head. "You are a pretty girl. But it is hidden beneath that hair of yours." With her forefinger, she lifted a section of Piety's greasy hair over her ear, "Listen to me, chicken." Piety looked intently into her one-time foster carer's eyes, "You *must* take care of yourself, and have a sense of pride. Hasn't your mum taught you these things?" Piety shook her head. "Has no one at the school offered to help?" Shake, shake. Aunty Nell kissed her teeth. "What's the world coming to when a child can go unheeded?" She kissed the top of Piety's head, and Piety remembered Mr Gadiid doing that to Aamina. It made her happy-cry. "You know, petal, you not going to make things right by cryin' and hidin', you know? Grown-ups don't know everything, why, your mammy is barely an adult herself and she been through some stuff too, I expect. You let your brother and your mum deal with their own issues, yeah? And focus on yourself."

She proceeded to give Piety a lecture on self-care and cleanliness. It was a lot of information, but Piety tried ever so hard to remember everything.

"Now, I think you should get along home. I am sure your mother will be worried. It is getting late."

Piety hadn't noticed that the sky was getting dull. Aunty Nell gave her some money for the return bus fare because she had none, and told her which bus stop to get the right bus from. Piety wasn't sure where she was. They hugged for a long time; not long enough for Piety, before heading their separate ways. Piety watched Aunty Nell until she disappeared around a corner.

When she pushed open the front door. Tommy was sitting on the window ledge drumming his heels against the wall.

"Got any sweets?"
"Where the hell have you been?" Mum charged in from the kitchen. "I needed you to get some shopping in."
"Pi, don't stand there like a shop dummy," Dad

rasped from his habitual seat in front of the television, "get us a beer from the fridge."

Heaving a sigh, she fetched her father's beer; at least he was home, she found a Fab lolly ice at the bottom of the freezer and gave it to Tommy. Mum slid a cigarette from a packet of Embassy Regal and lit it. She regarded her family as they licked, puffed, and guzzled. Now they had what they wanted, she no longer mattered. But Piety didn't mind anymore. Not so much anyway.

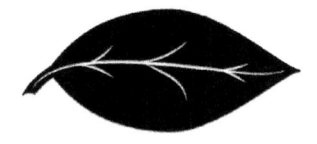

## Chapter Thirteen

Following Aunty Nell's instructions, Piety began to take a weekly bath.

"Pi! Get out of the fuckin' bath! Other people need to use the bathroom." Mum shouted and banged on the door.

Piety had knocked a nail into the door frame and used an old dressing gown cord to tie around the handle and the nail. It served as a perfunctory lock. Tommy and Dad were the first to let her be, all she had to say when they hammered on the door was, "I'm doing my feminine hygiene lady stuff." Aunty Nell said the words - *feminine hygiene* was sure to keep the menfolk at bay, it was stuff they didn't and didn't *want* to know about. To Piety, the two words conjured up images of beauty salons, nail polish, fresh deodorants, and perfumes. But it worked like magic when you said it. Aunty Nell had imposed on her how important this routine was, hygiene was about keeping all your bits, your cracks and crevices clean. She also noticed they never quite looked her in the eye when she came out of there. Mum was another matter.

"Who d'you think cares what you look like?" she'd snipe; like Caroline, thought Piety. "I bet you think you look gorgeous with your hair tied up," she sneered. "You're just a skinny kid with a spotty face." "Oh, here she is, saint fucking Pi."

There was a callousness there that Piety hadn't noticed when she was little, nor did she have the ability to comprehend. A mean-spiritedness. But she never retaliated, she made a vow to never be like her mum — she wanted to be like Miss Sparrow, or Nurse Halifax, or Aunty Nell. She continued to keep up her routine with determination, she washed her hair once a week and was amazed at how silky and shiny it actually was. Although her body was far cleaner than it had ever been, her clothes were the same. Having no money of her own, and Mum not thinking about anyone's needs but her own, Piety quickly grew out of her underwear. The pitiful shreds of washed-out grey looked more like dishrags than knickers. So, taking a leaf out of her favourite saint's book, she made her own. A sort of loincloth made from an old bed sheet she found screwed up and stuffed in the back of the airing cupboard. Being a skinny kid, as her mum put it, she was able to make more than one. It was slightly bulky beneath her school skirt, but she didn't mind. Unable to knot the two ends, she found a large pin in a kitchen drawer, left over from when her brother wore towelling nappies. In the school library, she'd learned these types of knickers were worn by Roman soldiers and gladiators as well as saints, she practised pronouncing the word.

That afternoon was P.E. Piety borrowed a kit from

Lost Property. Her ruse for claiming to be on her menstrual cycle had fallen apart after the P.E. teacher queried her *permanent state* one day. In the changing rooms, her classmates fell into bouts of hysterical laughter when they saw what lay beneath her uniform.

"What's all this commotion?" roared Miss Kearney as she flung back the changing room door. "Get your kits on and get outside. Now!"
"But miss," Rachel Lamb gasped between laughter, "have you seen what Scroggy is wearing?"
"She's got a nappy on, Miss," cried Caroline Ledsham.

Piety pulled on the shorts and Aertex shirt, both ill-fitting. She slipped on the black pumps and stared at the teacher as though nothing untoward had occurred. Miss Kearney looked at Piety's bulging shorts.

"Is this true?"
"No Miss," she replied calmly, "It's a subli…, a supli… supplemental. A loincloth. It's what the ancient Romans wore before modern underwear."
The teacher stared. "But why? A supplement for what?"

Piety couldn't tell her the real reason; she couldn't tell Miss and all the locker room that her knickers were shrivelled and too small. She couldn't tell them Mum hadn't bought her any new ones for years. It was bad enough being the poor kid without sharing details about your knickers, she could only imagine what they would say to that. Everyone in the changing room was staring, with smirks on their faces, even Carol, who had become friends with Rachael Lamb and by default, Caroline Ledsham. She caught Carol's eye, and her one-time friend rolled her eyes before turning away. Piety had a flash of inspiration.

She said simply, "It's history research."
"I haven't got time for this," Miss Kearney finally said, "Outside, the lot of you. I want two laps around the field."

Piety found herself at the rear on the running track as usual. Fifty yards ahead was the next slowest pupil; Diane Billington. Diane was slightly overweight and had eczema, but she still had friends. Ahead of *her* was a trio of girls, the main pack a few strides in front, but nobody was making much effort, despite the purple-faced exhortations of Miss Kearney from the sidelines.

Piety had no style when she ran. One of those kids who ran with arms flailing, feet flapping. That, or she *galumphed* along; as Miss Kearney described it, arms and legs uncoordinated. But for the first time, she began to enjoy the isolation, the feeling of the wind against her skin, the slap of her soles on grass and the slight ache in her calves and thighs. How had she not noticed this before? she wondered. She realised that much of her life was like this, always alone, always at the back. But being alone wasn't so bad, was it? You could think about anything you wanted, things other people thought stupid or weird. You didn't have to agree with things that you didn't really agree with privately. She could pretend that she was chasing a bad guy in *The Sweeny*, or that she was Scooby

Doo running from a ghost. This was fun. As she ran, a weight lifted with each fast exhalation, her chest swelled as she breathed deeper and deeper, and soon she felt light as a feather. Her hair was tied in two long bunches on either side of her head, and she liked the way they felt as the clean hair flapped and bounced against her neck. Ungainly as she was, twiggy arms and legs flapping and flailing as though she were a toddler, it was wonderfully liberating.

"Miss Scroggins!"

She saw Miss Kearney's purple-flushed face as she passed her and realised the woman must have been shouting for a while. The rest of the girls from her class stood in a delighted gaggle, staring from the sidelines. Piety was the only one on the track. Her heart pounded, her throat was dry, and her mouth tasted of iron. On the other side of the playing field, the boy's game of football had ceased to watch the goings on.

"Miss Scroggins. What in God's name are you doing?"

Piety, clutching the stitch in her side, tottered across to the teacher, "Sorry...Miss... didn't...hear you," she panted.
"I have been shouting for at least two minutes. Are you deaf as well as daft? The lesson is over, go and get a shower. All of you," she turned on the sniggering pack, "Now! Showers! Go!"

The teasing in the girl's changing room was unprecedented. Her clothes were strewn about the floor. Her bag had been chucked into the shower. Someone made a *waa-waa* baby noise that caused a ripple of chuckles. Caroline was combing her hair and humming. The humming became words, it was a *Bay City Rollers* song. Rachael joined in and soon everyone was singing about saying goodbye to their baby and crying.

She sat on the wooden bench in her loincloth made of bedsheet and one of Tommy's new vests and stared at the floor until everyone had gone. When Miss Kearney came to check the place was clear, she found Piety with her clothes bundled in her lap.

"Why are you still here? Come on, get a move on or you'll be late for your next lesson."

Why didn't you say anything? Why didn't you stop them? Every P.E. lesson my stuff gets thrown about and you do nothing. You know what's happening. You're a terrible teacher, Miss Kearney!

That was what she wanted to say. The words pressed themselves to the front of her tongue desperate to be spoken, so she clamped her teeth forming a cage around the words. When Piety had completed dressing, she turned to her teacher at the door.

"Do you have any kids, Miss?"

"No. I've enough to deal with, with you lot."

Piety thought it was just as well. But didn't say anything.

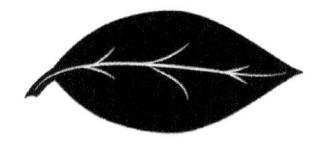

"I'm sorry."

Piety looked up into Aamina's face.
"I'm sorry for being mean, Piety. Can you forgive me?"

Aamina had approached her in the playground during the morning break. Piety was sitting on the bench where she had first spoken to her one-time friend. It was a beautiful day, the sky was cloudless, and a blackbird sang from the top of a chimney pot on one of the houses bordering the school grounds. Aamina said she was scared of Caroline and Rachael, they'd said stuff about her skin colour, and her parents had always told her to ignore these sorts of insults. It was hard enough anyway, being in another country without drawing further attention to oneself.

"I was a coward. I should have stood up for you when those girls made fun of you. I shouldn't have believed her, I didn't, I don't. But I was frightened of her. And…" She chewed her lip, "And it was me who put the soap in your bag. Please don't be angry," she said hurriedly. "I don't know what I was thinking. I meant it as a gift, as something nice, I didn't mean to say you needed a wash, I wasn't trying —"
"It's okay." Piety stood. "Honestly, Aamina. I was sad at first, but now we are friends again, I'm

happy. We are friends, aren't we?" The two girls hugged tight, and when they parted, Piety saw tears in her friend's eyes, so she hugged her again.

Aamina nodded and her voice came muffled from Piety's shoulder, "My parents were very cross with me when I told them. Mum said I had made you a stranger in your own land."
They parted, "What does that mean?" asked Piety. After a pause, Aamina gave a sad little apologetic smile, and said, "I don't know." They squinted at each other for a moment before laughing, "Oh, I have missed you, my funny friend," cried Aamina.

Piety was amazed at how she felt. Kind of full and light at the same time. As though she had swallowed the sun and it filled her so much that it couldn't help but seep from every pore of her being. Everyone would surely see it glowing from her like a beacon. Her heart seemed to skip in her chest and her stomach quivered delightfully. She couldn't stop grinning. They sat side-by-side catching up on lost days. Aamina had to get Piety to slow down as her excitement caused a torrent of words to come crashing out in disorder. Piety said that Mr Wright told her she had a 'racing car brain', and it made her talk too fast. Aamina said that Piety was always bursting with energy and ideas and that her dad, Mr Gadiid, said that was a great skill, but sometimes we must listen rather than talk. Piety showed Aamina her latest drawings. Her friend liked the one of the horses best.

The sound of shouting drew both girls' attention. It seemed a scuffle had broken out in the playground. Kids ran over, drawn like iron filings to a magnet.

Piety stood up and looked across the grey quadrangle. There's a particular sound when there's a schoolyard fight, a kind of localised chant followed by jeering and cheering that is instantly recognised by the pupils and staff of that school. This wasn't that. Aamina placed her hand on her arm,

"Piety, stay. Don't get involved."
"But someone is being bullied. *It's not right.*"

The small knot of figures undulated back and forth as whoever was at the centre was buffeted. Piety's arrival went unnoticed. Most pupils were taller than her and she had to stand on her toes to see over the shoulders of two boys. In the centre, she saw Aaron Brockley. His face was puffy, blotched red and white, like a funny colour panda, she mused. The front of his hair stood on end; a startled thatch, but whether by design or sweat, she couldn't tell.

"You're a little worm, Broccoli. A snitch and a shitty worm." The voice of Caroline Ledsham boomed.

Piety saw the girl, who was at least a head taller than Aaron, jab her finger in his face. The boy couldn't back off, Caroline's cronies had him hemmed in. He looked scared. Like Piety, Aaron had not grown much since primary school. Caroline, on the other hand, was what Dad referred to as 'a hormone monster'. Big, muscular, busty, with a mouth to match. In her mind's eye bloomed images one after the other, memories she didn't know she had, as though her brain had made a film she hadn't seen, or taken a series of snapshots without her realising — *click,* she saw Aaron getting lifts to and from school in his dad's shiny car, and then, *click*, he wasn't. She saw him with lots of friends, and then, *click,* none. She saw him hanging around the edge of the playground in scuffed shoes and eating alone in the canteen. The way that he had turned from her at the bus stop the time Caroline and Rachael had bullied her, that look on his face. Those watching were grinning hyenas. Baying for more, roaring for someone's blood, because, she realised, if you were one of the crowd you weren't on the receiving end of a good hiding. Piety couldn't see a single one who wasn't enjoying the spectacle of a boy being beaten by a girl. She didn't see the slap but heard it.

"Fuck off, you fat cow!" Aaron yipped.
"Or what? You'll go running to the teachers like a wittle baby? Waa, waa!"

Piety couldn't imagine Aaron Brockley telling tales. It must be a mistake. She squeezed her way through the press of bodies.

"Don't think you can get one over on me, you little fart." Caroline slapped his face again. "Snitch again," slap, "and I'll flatten you," slap. "Aaron *Broccoli*. You even smell like broccoli. You stink like mashed sprouts n cabbage. Fuckin' little fart."
"Leave him alone." The words popped out before she had time to think.
An 'ooh' rippled round the crowd. Next to her, a large kid from the year above, gave her a shove, "Shut it, grease-ball."

Piety ignored him, and stepped forwards, placing herself between the two adversaries.

"Leave him alone, Caroline. He hasn't done anything wrong."
"Look, it's the stinky povvo's sticking together," Caroline sneered, "Fuck off, Scraggy."

But when the bigger girl attempted to push Piety aside, she found a suddenly immovable force between herself and her victim. Piety planted her feet. She rocked sideways, but would not budge, she was Ann Wilson from *Grange Hill* confronting the school bully. She was DI Jack Regan of *The Sweeney* fighting criminals.

"Need a girl to fight your battles, Broccoli?" someone jeered.
"Get lost, Pi," Aaron hissed. "I don't need your help."

But he'd used her name, sort of. She turned her head a little. Saw the snot on his blazer. The bright red handprint on his cheek. His bag emptied on the floor, trampled and gritty, the contents scattered.

"You're bigger than either of us. You're a nasty, mean girl, Caroline Ledsham. Go and pick on someone your own size."
The spectators laughed uproariously. Someone mimicked in a high-pitched, sing-song voice, "You're a mean girl, Caroline," and everyone laughed some more.
"Smack her, Caro!" a girl called.
"Yeah! Smack the smell out of 'em!"

Caroline glared down at Piety. Piety's tummy roiled, but she swallowed down the fear and thought of

Saint Peter. She clasped her hands and tilted her head to look wide-eyed up at the bigger girl. She didn't know what effect it would have. She didn't know why she was doing it. She couldn't help herself. If the bigger girl laughed at her, then she might make her forget about Aaron, she might call them names and walk off thinking Piety was being her usual odd self, and that would be okay. She was wearing one of her loincloths today. It was super comfortable and comforting. It made her feel safe. Made her feel like she had all the saints and angels on her side. The bigger girl was in the wrong and a bully, and you had to stand up to bullies. Saint Peter would be proud of her.

Caroline punched her hard in the face. Piety staggered, more from shock than pain, arms flailing for balance. Little lights exploded in her vision. She'd actually hit her! Piety couldn't believe it. Her knees did a comic wobble. The circle of onlookers gone silent, expanded leaving a space which she staggered around before falling. She landed heavily on her elbows and knees, managed to somehow turn herself and flopped down. Faces overlapped and kept going in and out of focus. Squiggly purple worms darted around in front of her eyes. Her head felt the size of a beachball.

"Shit!" someone said. And then everyone scarpered.

A beautiful brown face floated like a balloon somewhere to her right.
"Is that you, Madonna?" Piety quavered.

She shook her head and blinked her eyes.

Suddenly they were all gone. All except Aamina, and Aaron who looked down at her with a frown.

"Are you alright?" he said. She tried to nod but her head went swirly. "I…" he started. "You're *weird*, Piety Scroggins." And he too, ran for it.

Aamina helped her to her feet. The playground was empty. "That was shocking. I have never seen a girl punch someone. Are you okay?"
Piety squeezed her eyes shut. Opened them wide, and rubbed her cheek, "I think so."
Heading indoors, Aamina said, "You know, he is right, to a degree."
"Who?"
"That boy, Aaron. You are weird." But she was smiling fondly.
"I know," Piety nodded, "I know."

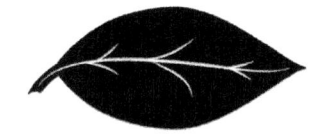

# Chapter Fourteen

Something weird happened. Piety was walking down Kirk Road after school this one day, the sun trying to peek through cracks in the clouds and little kids, who got home from school earlier, were already playing out. Because of the curve in her road, she could see her house, smack bang in the middle, from quite a way off.

The front door opened, and a figure stepped out. Dad followed and she could see Mum leaning out the doorway. She could recognise Mum and Dad from this distance, but not the other person. She could hear Dad shouting, but not the words. Piety stopped walking and stared. The visitor turned to face Dad and said something. Dad's arm came up, fist bunched. Then stopped when the man waved a piece of paper at him. Mum hurried out to the pavement and tried to grab the piece of paper, but before she could, it was folded and stuffed into a pocket. The visitor pointed a finger at Dad, wagging it like he was telling him off. It looked funny seeing Dad being talked to like he was a big kid. The man seemed familiar, but Piety didn't think it could be him.

People on the road had stopped to stare. Mrs Lawler from across the road stood outside her door with her arms folded, she didn't even try to hide the fact that she was watching. Piety ducked into someone's gateway when Dad looked around. She peeked around the straggly privet hedge. The man got into an old car, and she heard the engine start, the car was coming this way. Piety hunkered down and watched from her hiding place. A little grey Anglia with scabby rust patches went past and Piety saw the frowning profile of Mr Wright. She clutched at her chest. What did he want? How did he know where she lived? Had she done something wrong at school? Think, think. She couldn't remember. She was sure that she was always good and worked hard in art class. She continued a slow walk home, worried about what would be said. Scared that her parents were going to give her the shouting of a lifetime. She felt sick.

One stride up from the pavement to the front door. Inside. Quiet. Then she heard the low murmur of her parents in the kitchen. She closed the door softly as she could. Tommy appeared at the top of the stairs and waved her up.

"You never guess what," he said.
"What?" Piety stood in the middle of the bedroom as her brother looked out the window.
"This bloke turned up and shouted at Mum and Dad."
"What for? Who?"
"Dunno. He said he was the witch's son and he'd heard all about how they were treating you!" he leapt onto his bed. "Dad should have hit him. He could have taken him, dead easy."

"What d'you mean, witch's son? I don't understand."
"Y'know, the old biddy who lives on the corner? The witch? He said," and her brother did an impersonation of a man's voice. "My mother lives round here. Mrs Wright, you know her? On the corner? And I know you treat your kids wrong. I'm gonna write to Social Services, see?" Tommy's normal voice resumed. "And he showed them some paperwork."
"What was it?" Piety felt sicker and sicker.
"Dunno. Didn't see it. I was up on the top of the stairs earwiggin'."

Piety sat heavily on her bed. A spring went clunk then a twang. Social Services? Did that mean she'd be taken away again? Did that mean Tommy would? She honestly did not know how she felt about that. Mr Wright hadn't said anything since their talk in his stockroom. He had been his usual self. But the weirdest thing to her was, Mr Wright was the witch's son.

Mum made tea. It was only sausages and mash, but it was good. No one spoke at all throughout the meal. Dad washed the dishes in silence. Piety felt like someone had plugged the whole house into a faulty socket so that it buzzed with expectant electricity. When nine o'clock came, Dad said it was time for bed. Tommy protested and Dad went scarlet, so Piety and Tommy legged it up the stairs.

Nothing was ever said about Mr Wright's visit to the house. Her parents did not go out to the pub that week, or the next. Piety and Tommy had dinner money for school every day. A packet of knickers appeared on Piety's bed one day, new socks on Tommy's the next. Mr Wright never mentioned it in school. It was as though nothing had occurred. Piety thought she might have imagined the whole episode if it wasn't for the fact that her parents were behaving differently. Not hugely. But they seemed to want to keep a distance between themselves and her, especially Mum, who carefully asked if anything had happened at school. Mum and Dad still swore and shouted, but they'd suddenly stop as if they had caught themselves. They spent more time together, huddled around the TV or kitchen table, whispering. It reminded Piety of pupils who were on report. It finally dawned on her what the atmosphere was, the quiet, and the behaviour of her parents. Shame.

The letterbox flapped. Mum dashed to the front window, hiding behind the curtain and peeping through the nets. This had become a regular thing with Mum now. She had become quite jumpy and would keep checking out the window to see if anyone was watching, and Piety sometimes heard her mutter about Mrs Lawler. But Mrs Lawler hadn't done anything. Piety stood on the other side of the window mirroring her mum's stance. The gate screeched. A brown figure bumbled past, rolling a little with the difficult walk that comes with age. Piety recognised the wrinkled toffee features from the side. The word witch, formed on her tongue. But Mum muttered something else, it sounded like "Mrs friggin' Wright."

"It's for you," she mumbled to Piety and left the room with no explanation.

The reused brown envelope, scrunched and sellotaped, contained a troll doll. It had golden-yellow hair and wore a tiny felt white shirt and a bright yellow felt skirt with shoulder straps. She stared into its inky polished eyes. It was brand new.

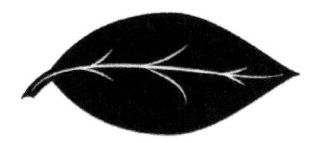

## Chapter Fifteen

Two weeks later, the story of the 'fight' between Caroline Ledsham and two other kids faded to make way for new gossip. Piety still found herself alone in classes; no one would partner up with her for games, and she was mostly ignored now — which was better. She had become meaningless to the bullies, although there was still the occasional snide remark. When she turned up for Remedial maths, she found that someone had placed a single chocolate on her desk, no one owned up to doing it.

Mr Wright set the task for the day; create a poster and flyer for any campaign they wanted. Piety had seen something on Blue Peter for their latest appeal which she wanted to try. Everyone got busy with sketching ideas, Mr Wright had taught them that you can't make a finished product straight away, you must plan, come up with designs, and make small versions before creating the final article. Piety had a whole table to herself, so she spread out her papers, pencils, and paints. Someone pulled out the chair opposite. She looked up, there stood Aaron Brockley.

"Hi," he muttered.
"Hi?"

What did he want? She saw Mr Wright look over at her table, he kept watch for a moment then headed over to his record player.

"Okay to sit here?" Aaron said.
Piety shrugged.

They didn't say anything else for ages. Both worked in silence on their individual projects. When they dipped their paintbrushes into the red paint at the same time, they stared at each other for a moment, and then Aaron withdrew his brush and waited for Piety to be done. With his head down, busy, Aaron spoke.

"Sorry. Y'know. It was stupid. All that at Beacon Park." Piety did not respond. "I didn't mean it. I mean, kind of, at the time. But, I wasn't thinking, but I know now, I get it." He still had not looked at her. "And thanks. For sticking up for me, y'know?"

Their paintbrushes were motionless. The classroom was a susurration of pencils and brushes on paper against a background of *Angels with Dirty Faces* by Sham 69. She looked at him. Saw his hair flopped down over his eyes, he used to always have the latest, trendy haircuts. She noticed a food stain on his tie and the dirt under his nails. When he met her stare, she couldn't work out what he was thinking, he looked angry and mean, and scared. She had not noticed before, but Aaron had the most amazing green eyes and little freckles on his nose. Piety looked back at her work and continued to paint and chewed her lip. What if he was about to start all over again? What if it was a...what did DS Regan call it? A con; what if he was pretending to apologise? Too many 'what ifs' to fit in her head, she didn't know what to say, because now she understood that sometimes people say things they don't mean. And sometimes we must listen and not talk.

Aaron spoke so quietly that she almost didn't hear. "My dad left us."

He said nothing else after that. She wasn't sure, but Aaron might have been about to cry. His cheeks looked swollen and hot; the way her brother's used to when he was a toddler. He rested his forehead on the palm of his left hand as he continued to make meaningless marks on the paper, so she couldn't see his face anymore.

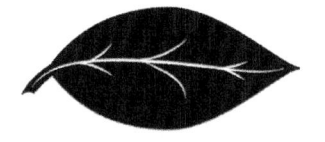

It was nearing the end of the school year. Summer loitered on the horizon. The laburnum trees along the inside of the school railings, bore large, hanging bunches of bright yellow flowers, the scent of mown grass filled the air and the distant hum of the mower soothed as the sports field was mown for the last time this term. Aamina had become Piety's best and only friend, but Piety decided that one best friend was worth five Carol Beverleys. The insults and catcalls had become background to her

— she was used to it finally. The bus queue was frantic and tangled as usual. Dense with kids as though there wasn't pavement enough on either side. A particularly tall sixth-form boy accidentally knocked her with his bag as he pushed in front.

"Sos, mate," he offered. Then seemed to do a double take. "Hey, aren't you the kid that huge girl knocked out?" When does it ever end? Piety groaned inwardly. The blush seemed to begin in her toes and flamed up to her hair roots. She nodded. "What a bitch!" he said. "She must be twice your size." Piety gawped. "See ya."

Piety and Aamina looked at each other and mouthed, *Wow.*
A small white car pulled up in front of the bus stop.

"Hey! Piety! Aamina!" She saw Aaron Brockley stick his head out of the passenger window. "Wanna lift?"

Hesitant, Piety and Aamina approached the vehicle.

"Seriously?" she ducked her head to look at who was driving. A tired, sad-looking woman, older than her mum, but still fashionably dressed. The woman looked at her.
"Come on kids, get in quick, I'm blocking the bus."

Piety and Aamina told Aaron's mum where they lived. She said it wasn't too far out of the way, now they'd moved. The car jerked a lot, as though it was silently coughing, but no one minded, except Mrs Brockley who sometimes cursed quietly as she shifted the gearstick. Aaron twisted around in his seat; ignoring his mum's weary pleas to sit still.

"We got a new car. What d'you think?" he smiled. Aamina said it was very nice. Piety nodded in agreement. "' Course, it's not *new* new," Aaron said. "It's second-hand. But we can't afford to buy new cars anymore."
Mrs Brockley turned her head quickly, "Aaron! That's private!" she yanked the wheel and stamped on the accelerator.
"Piety doesn't mind, do you Pi?"

The journey was shorter than on the bus. Piety and Aamina stayed silent most of the time, occasionally looking at each other and shrugging. Aamina got out first, leaving Piety alone with Aaron and Mrs Brockley, Piety pressed the palm of her hand to the window and stared at her friend standing on the pavement until she could see her no more. They arrived in Kirk Road after Piety had asked Mrs Brockley to drop her off at the end on the main road, and Mrs Brockley refused, she'd 'do no such thing'. Piety didn't want Aaron and his sad mum to see where she lived. She didn't want her parents to see her get out of someone's car.

"Thank you, Mrs Brockley," she said as she closed the car door.
"You're welcome, Piety," she replied and turned up the radio.
"You can have a lift every day if you like, can't she Mum?"
"We'll see."
"Do you wanna go to the pictures in the hols?" Aaron said.

Piety felt her palms were slick with sweat, and her stomach felt as though it had curled into a tight ball like a kitten, but she asked anyway.

"Are you my friend now, Aaron?" She felt like she was six not twelve and a half.
"Sure," he smiled. "So?"
"I'd like that," Piety said.

He waved as the car pulled away. And for the first time since she could remember, Aaron Brockley looked genuinely happy. The car jerked away in a plume of fumes and to the sound of Abba singing *Take a Chance on Me*.


The End

# ABOUT THE AUTHOR

E.V Faulkner is the pen name of a multi-genre author.

Also by E.V Faulkner

Rottnest

/ Saint Peter's Knickers

Printed in Great Britain
by Amazon